Kondo wa zettai ni jama shimasen! Novel 4
by Soratani Reina, Harukawa Haru
© 2022 SORATANI REINA, HARUKAWA HARU/
GENTOSHA COMICS INC.
All rights reserved.
Original Japanese edition published in 2022 by
GENTOSHA COMICS Inc.
English translation rights arranged worldwide with
GENTOSHA COMICS Inc. through Digital Catapult Inc., Tokyo.

Seven Seas press and purchase enquiries can be sent to
Marketing Manager Lianne Sentar at press@gomanga.com.
Information regarding the distribution and purchase of
digital editions is available from Digital Manager CK Russell
at digital@gomanga.com.

Seven Seas and the Seven Seas logo are trademarks of
Seven Seas Entertainment. All rights reserved.

Follow Seven Seas Entertainment online at
sevenseasentertainment.com.

TRANSLATION: Molly Lee
ADAPTATION: Lorin Christie
COVER DESIGN: M. A. Lewife
LOGO DESIGN: George Panella
INTERIOR DESIGN: Clay Gardner
INTERIOR LAYOUT: Jennifer Elgabrowny
PROOFREADER: Meg van Huygen
COPY EDITOR: Jade Gardner
LIGHT NOVEL EDITOR: Cypress Catwell
PREPRESS TECHNICIAN: Melanie Ujimori, Jules Valera
MANAGING EDITOR: Alyssa Scavetta
EDITOR-IN-CHIEF: Julie Davis
ASSOCIATE PUBLISHER: Adam Arnold
PUBLISHER: Jason DeAngelis

ISBN: 978-1-63858-764-4
Printed in Canada
First Printing: December 2023
10 9 8 7 6 5 4 3 2 1

I Swear I Won't Bother You AGAIN!

NOVEL 4

WRITTEN BY

Reina Soratani

ILLUSTRATED BY

Haru Harukawa

Airship

Seven Seas Entertainment

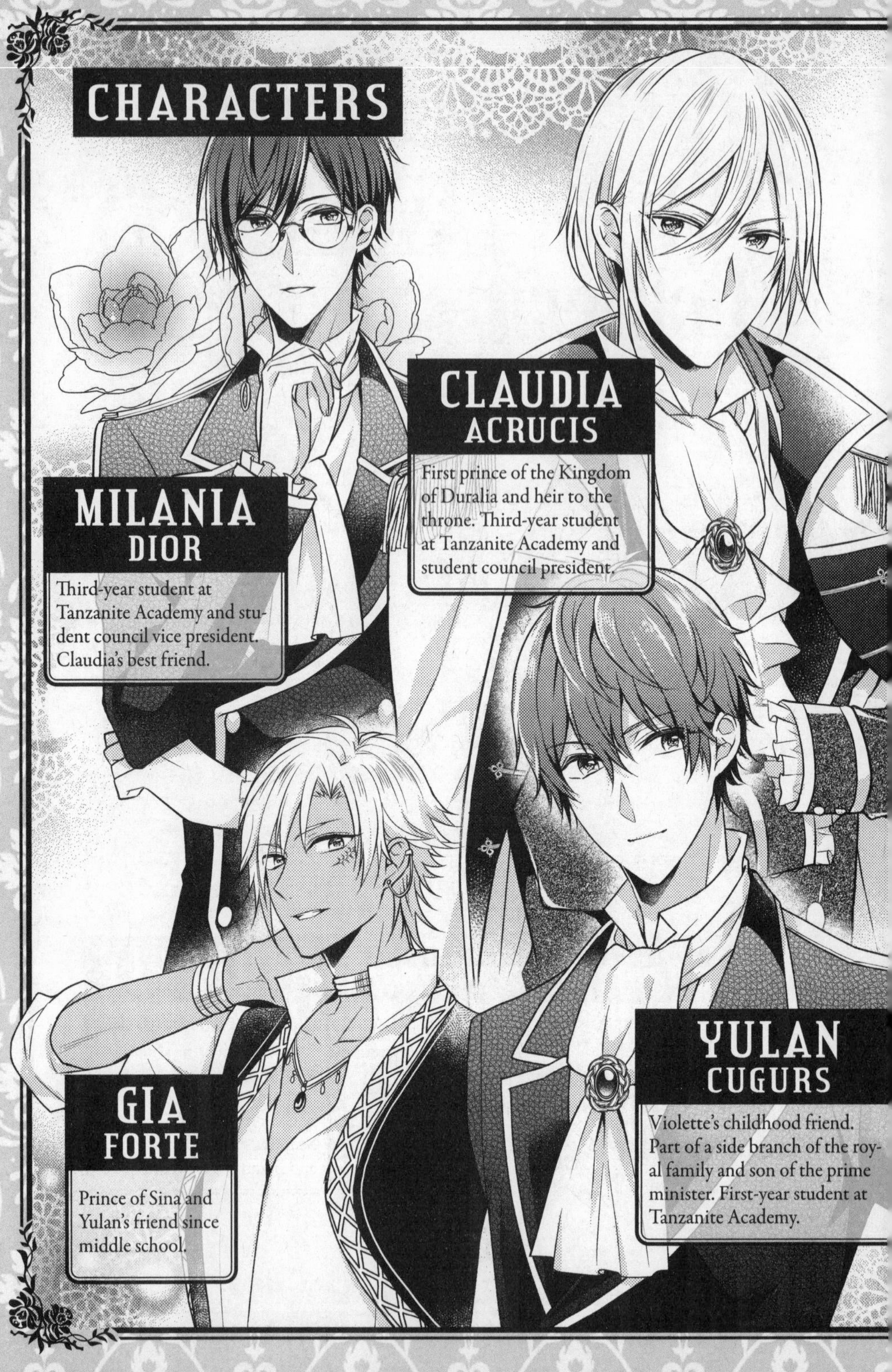
CHARACTERS
CLAUDIA ACRUCIS
First prince of the Kingdom of Duralia and heir to the throne. Third-year student at Tanzanite Academy and student council president.
MILANIA DIOR
Third-year student at Tanzanite Academy and student council vice president. Claudia's best friend.
YULAN CUGURS
Violette's childhood friend. Part of a side branch of the royal family and son of the prime minister. First-year student at Tanzanite Academy.
GIA FORTE
Prince of Sina and Yulan's friend since middle school.

MARYJUNE VAHAN

Second daughter of Duke Vahan. Violette's half sister and first-year student at Tanzanite Academy.

MARIN

The maid who serves Violette.

ROSETTE MEGAN

Princess of the neighboring country of Lithos and second-year student at Tanzanite Academy.

VIOLETTE REM VAHAN

Eldest daughter of Duke Vahan, imprisoned for the attempted murder of her half sister. Sent back in time. Second-year student at Tanzanite Academy.

⇥Table of Contents⇤

141 Birds of a Feather, like It or Not

YULAN ARRIVED HOME before sunrise. He was glad to be back ahead of schedule, but his body ached from all that sitting. The slightest stretch made his joints pop all over. Thus, he decided he'd nap until his usual waking hour. This would be nowhere near enough to cure his fatigue, alas. When he awoke a few hours later, his parents suggested he take the day off from school, but he spurred his leaden body into action. Year-end exams were fast approaching. He could have studied at home, but school was the only place he'd get to see Violette.

Agh, my neck...

He must have slept on it wrong because the muscle protested at the slightest movement. Of all the aches and pains in his limbs and back, this one was the worst. No amount of stretching or massaging helped. Suppressing a grimace, he cheerfully greeted each nameless, faceless acquaintance he passed in the hall.

At his classroom, Yulan found Gia at his desk, chomping on an absurdly large loaf of bread. An uncommon sight, but at this point, hardly surprising.

"Bah arreddeh?"

"Don't talk with your mouth full."

"*Mmgh!* ...Back already?"

"I said I'd be back today, didn't I?"

"That ya did."

The canines that peeked out with every bite of bread gave Gia a wolfish air. Though his boyish good looks might suggest a more domesticated breed, Yulan had known him long enough to understand that he was only loyal to his own interests. While Yulan identified as an unethical person and would never claim otherwise, Gia didn't so much as *think* about ethics.

Birds of a feather flock together, as the saying went; Yulan didn't much enjoy being lumped in with someone like Gia, but he couldn't deny this boy understood him far better than his own parents.

"Anything happen while I was gone?"

"Mmm, not really... Oh, but your princess came askin' for ya at one point."

"*What?!*"

"Relax, would you? I tried to ask her for deets, but she said it was nothin' and ran off... C'mon, don't be so dramatic. She's not dead, y'know."

"Shut up."

Gia scarcely batted a lash at Yulan's crestfallen face, as if to suggest he'd anticipated his disappointment. Meanwhile, Yulan's mind was a whirlwind of directionless emotion. He knew he would have had no choice but to skip school that day, even if he'd known Violette would come asking for him, yet he still cursed himself for it. He understood intellectually it was beyond his control and he'd needed to go, but there was no way to bring his heart into line.

"Uggghhh... I wish I could clone myself..."

"D'you realize how dumb ya sound right now?"

Even if he *could* clone himself, they'd all just argue over who got to stay behind. Though it was an important undertaking, that didn't mean he wanted to do it; if another version of himself existed, he would pass the buck. And for all that was holy, the last thing this world needed was more people like him. They would probably start a war to form their own country just for Violette.

"...Well? Anything else?"

After a moment of wallowing, Yulan looked up at Gia, his eyes like blazing suns. Their sparkle, soft and sweet like crisp morning rays, could harden suddenly and become the glint of light on the edge of a blade. When his lips curled boyishly, who could imagine that so much hatred and resentment lay beneath?

He was, above all, *sincere*. That was not to be mistaken for purity or innocence. Any dainty flower who thought him harmless wouldn't survive the winter.

"Far as I know, it all played out exactly how ya wanted," Gia replied.

"Yeah? Good."

"I'm guessin' your little trip worked out?"

"If it hadn't, I wouldn't be here."

"Glad to hear it, then."

The next thing he knew, Gia had polished off the last bite of his bread with an irreverent smirk. All this time, he never saw Yulan as anything more than entertainment—and that would never change. He was the sort of scoundrel who evaluated other people's lives solely for his own amusement. Now, his eyes glittered with excitement at the prospect of Yulan's herbicide choking the life from a beautiful bloom.

"...You know, you're more of a monster than I could ever be."

"Oh, I know."

"And," Yulan added, "you really piss me off."

Gia laughed at him.

142 Behind It All

BETWEEN CLASSES, Yulan jogged straight to Violette's classroom. She was never one to linger there, and lately she'd started spending more time socializing. He'd need to hurry. Ideally, he would've liked to run at full speed, but the halls were filled with other students and forced him to slow his pace. Aggravating, yes, but the crowds also slowed Violette down. He bumped into her at the foot of the staircase, so it wasn't all bad.

"Vio!"

"Yulan! You're back?"

"Yeah, just got back this morning. Gia said you were asking for me?"

"Oh...yes, erm, I wanted to speak with you."

"Sorry I wasn't there..."

"You have nothing to apologize for! I'm the one who turned up unannounced."

She was her usual self—his kind, beautiful goddess. The whole train ride home, he'd been desperate to see her as soon as possible. The past few days without her had felt like an eternity;

the journey itself was comfortable enough, and yet the entire time he'd been gripped with a desire as fundamental as hunger or thirst. Now here stood the very girl whose smile he'd been craving...and yet...

Why did something about her feel...*off*...?

"...Hey, Vio?"

"Hmm?"

"Did something happen while I was gone?"

Her complexion was ashen, but that was hardly uncommon for her. With Violette, pale was the norm. Even her hair was painted in soft watercolors. The only thing rosy about her was her lips, which flushed a bewitchingly coral red. Sure, they were a little chapped today, but that wasn't what had given Yulan pause.

Her soft smile, her gentle voice—it all felt fake. In fact, it reminded him of the previous timeline. The last time he saw *that* Violette, they had all called her a murderess, and she'd resigned herself to her crime...

"What's wrong? What happened? Are you hurt? Who was it? *What did they do?!*"

Before he knew it, he was gripping her shoulders. In her widened eyes, he could see the reflection of a madman...but though she was clearly panicked, he couldn't stop. He was reliving the terror of that fateful day all over again.

Unbeknownst to him, Violette had been driven into a jealous rage, then imprisoned for attempted murder. From that tragedy, he'd learned that he needed more than love to pick up on the important details. He'd started keeping close tabs on her until he could detect the faintest fluctuations...partly for her sake and partly to comfort his own anxiety.

The last time he saw her before he left on his trip, he noticed her smile. It proved genuine to all his senses—sincere delight tinged with a hint of embarrassment. This smile, by contrast, was an emotionless mask, like a reenactment of remembered feeling. What had happened over the scant few days he was absent? Who was behind it, and why had they chosen the precise days he wasn't around? Had everything burned to ash the moment he glanced away?

Right when I'd arranged it all perfectly... Right when I thought we were finally going to be okay...!

Was he too late? Would it all be for naught? No. He couldn't let that happen at *any* cost. He hadn't achieved anything yet—he hadn't finished a single thing!

"Yu...lan...? What's—?"

"Vio, there's something we need to discuss."

The shadows of his past faded from his mind, but in their place brewed a maelstrom of fear, confusion, and paranoia. Before Violette could recover from her alarm, before she disappeared behind that fake smile again, he blurted out his demands. He needed to reach her before her brain could process, and remember things, and put the pieces together. Before she decided to abandon hope, he needed to tell her she didn't have to.

"It's really important, so it might take a while...but it's something you need to hear."

His tone was imploring—painfully pressing, but nothing that could be considered harsh. On the contrary, it sounded as though *he* might shatter if she were to say no. The intensity on his face was chilling, yet heartbreaking at the same time. She must have sensed he was close to tears.

"Of course. I promise, I'll listen to every word," she told him, smiling gently, in the sort of voice one used to reassure a child.

That was all it took to breathe life back into Yulan's heart. He let out the breath he hadn't realized he was holding. The tension in his body drained away, and his hands fell away from her shoulders.

"Gah—I'm so sorry! Did I hurt you?"

"No, no, I'm fine. You just startled me, that's all."

"Oh...right...yes. Really sorry about that."

"Hee hee! I think that was the most panicked I've ever seen you."

"Any way you could forget it ever happened...?"

He buried his face in his hands, and as his emotions stabilized, the embarrassment set in. He could feel his ears burning red, but it was too late now.

"So, when shall we meet up?" Violette asked. "If it's going to take a while, we may not have enough time between classes."

"Preferably sometime after school. Do you have plans? Tomorrow would work too."

His bashful cheek-scratching was such a stark contrast to his earlier behavior that she couldn't help but smile. "Oh, I'm free today, so—"

"Wait... *Wait!*"

The conversation stopped dead. The air froze around them as their eyes lit on the sudden intruder. Now Violette was more confused than ever before. Her eyes narrowed with suspicion as she called:

"Maryjune...?"

"I'm sorry to interrupt, but...um...I overheard, and..."

Yulan wasn't especially upset about the eavesdropping. This staircase was by no means a popular hangout, but it saw a fair amount of foot traffic. It was reasonable to assume anyone could be listening in. Were he concerned about such things, he would have moved to an empty classroom. Maryjune's *faux pas* was thinking she had the right to barge into any conversation she happened to overhear.

"The truth is, after school today...*I* need to speak to Yulan."

"*Excuse* me?" He responded with no filter whatsoever, distrust and annoyance plain to hear. For a moment his heart stopped—but thankfully Violette seemed completely distracted by Maryjune's statement.

"Um...like I said, I was wondering if I could get a moment of your time later..."

"Hold on, back up—"

"*Please!*"

Maryjune clasped her hands at her chest like a praying angel. Unfortunately for her, Yulan was an atheist. He worshipped Violette alone. Maryjune sounded like she was going to cry, but her tears were worthless and powerless to move him. All he felt was disgust. Yulan could blow her off without a shred of guilt. Violette felt differently.

"I'm fine with it if Yulan is," she told her, pasting on a flawless smile. He recognized it as a shield she raised whenever she was confronted with something that scared her. "I can wait until tomorrow."

"Th-thank you so much!"

This was enough of a green light for Maryjune. She didn't bother to confirm it with Yulan himself. In fact, she didn't even seem to realize her sister was shielding against any threat, let alone that she herself was the threat in question.

Hatred would have been natural; Violette had at one point despised Maryjune to the point of homicide, and for good reason. It would come as no surprise if those feelings were buried but alive. But this reaction was borne of fear. She'd spotted a snake.

"Okay, see you later!"

Pearly white hair fluttered away in a hurry, but Yulan was more concerned about Violette. Beneath her bangs, her gaze was tilted diagonally downward. Her fake smile was even more unnerving for its beauty.

"I'm sorry you didn't get a say in that, Yulan."

"Nah, don't worry about me. Seriously though, did something—"

The sound of the bell drowned out his voice, driving a wedge between them. With discomfort lodged in his throat, he could only watch as Violette waved and walked away. He went back to class alone, the endless questions on his mind gradually shifting into frustration at Maryjune. As he contemplated his resentment for her, he didn't suspect that a different pearly-haired woman could be behind it all.

143 Out Loud

ANGER TENDED to subside over time, but Yulan was an exception to the rule. By the time the final bell rang, his irritation had grown twofold. Every voice grated on his ears, and whenever something moved within his line of sight, he had to stop himself from glaring at it.

Most people only knew him as the type who never got mad at anything; Gia was more likely to notice he was angry, but also more likely not to care. This knowledge drove his frustration to spiral further out of control.

What enraged him most of all was that Maryjune, the *source* of said rage, was blithely unaware of it. There was a difference between good cheer and outright disregard for others. Sure, it was likely a product of her upbringing, but it took a certain level of natural temperament to believe without question that the world revolved around her. Completely oblivious.

"Yulan...!"

She ran into the empty classroom, her expression on the cusp of tears. With her pale, pretty little face, eyes glistening, her voice calling his name with such anguish—in his shoes, most people would have felt compelled to come to her aid. If this pearly white angel shed a tear, the rest of the world would surely fret and cry right along with her. Sadly, Yulan had no interest in tears unless they came from his goddess. The only thing he felt toward Maryjune was growing annoyance.

"What?"

"Oh...um..."

He felt no concern for her, made no attempt at small talk to reassure her. It didn't occur to him to do so. This conversation was going to be difficult for her—so what? *Get to the point and get it over with.* At his prompting, she faltered, unsure where to begin. She was probably trying to think of the best way to explain it. Unfortunately for her, he already knew why she was here.

Well, he didn't know for *certain*, but he had an educated guess. He'd been the one who put that pout on her face to begin with.

"While you were away, um...the study group met up like usual, but..."

As she stammered, he became convinced that his little seeds had taken root. Granted, this was the worst possible timing, though it appeared to have been very effective. While he knew she was reckless enough to make a beeline straight to him about it, he hadn't anticipated that it would happen this soon. Still, his plan was a success. If only her timing hadn't spoiled his opportunity to talk to Violette, he could have celebrated it.

"I overheard them talking about...um...the way you feel about me."

They said Yulan didn't like Maryjune.

That he found her unpleasant.

Rumor had it he thought her mother was a dirty, thieving harlot, and he scorned her with a passion.

With every barbed remark she repeated, Maryjune's expression twisted in pain, her gaze imploring, as if the words escaping her throat tore it. How irritating, Yulan couldn't find it in himself to even fake a smile.

The discord he'd sown was not especially significant. They were the kind of petty rumors that would wither away with time... unless, of course, someone with a green thumb had a mind to cultivate them. Too weak to grow in barren soil, but when fertilized with a strong sense of moral integrity, closed-mindedness, and a dash of curiosity, such rumors would soon bloom.

"There must be some mistake, right, Yulan? You'd never—"

"I never said any of that."

Instantly her face lit up with joy, as if to suggest she'd never once doubted him. Had she already forgotten the anxiety she'd felt a moment prior? It was a wonder how she wasn't completely crippled by her own stupidity. She was free to believe him or not, but it wasn't his problem.

All he ever said was that Maryjune made him uncomfortable— an embarrassed admission he couldn't help but let slip with a guilty smile on his face. Each person who heard it interpreted it as they saw fit, then passed it down. From there it evolved, growing roots and leaves and thorns until it was practically unrecognizable.

He had intentionally included some of Violette's secret fans in that group too. It was too risky to involve her directly in any disparagement of her sister, so he carefully selected only those who had the good sense to worship her from a distance. Compared to the handful of uncultured hangers-on in her former posse, there were far more of these covert admirers than she would ever know about.

Yulan didn't know the full extent of how this flower had blossomed. Gia wouldn't know, either; he was never one to keep an ear out for rumors. Poor Maryjune made it sound as though word had spread almost exactly the way he'd imagined.

His lips curled into a smile—not from delight or amusement but satisfaction at a job well done. From here, it would be a trivial act to bring the little angel crashing down to rock bottom. Without an ounce of warmth or mercy, he continued, "I *thought* it, obviously, but I never said it out loud."

144 Gold Burns Blue

"H UH...?"

Yulan's words put a crack in that dazzling smile. She froze stiff, and as all trace of joy drained from her face, he felt his own smile grow.

"It may be true, but I at least have the good sense to keep it to myself. Sure, you're only sisters on paper, but I still wouldn't want Vio to have to hear it."

"What are you—why would you—?! *Why?*"

Her expression slowly twisted in horror, and at that moment he realized she truly hadn't grasped a thing. She wasn't just blinkered—she was utterly blind. He had to wonder if she'd lived her entire life with her eyes closed. The world around her had been painstakingly arranged so that she'd never need to open them—so that she'd never try. With the grace of a ballerina, she thoughtlessly trampled everything in her way.

"Sleeping with a married man, having his baby, and then swooping in to remarry him right after his first wife dies? If that's not thievery, I don't know what is. Fact of the matter is, she *is* dirty and a harlot to boot. She's reaping what she sowed."

As he laid out that witch's deeds, it reminded him why he loathed her. There were many terms for it—mistress, concubine—but that was merely high society's way of dressing up adultery. These men had the money and power to do as they liked (and occasionally the lack of an heir necessitated it), and so they mistakenly believed that it was *permissible*. Wealthy elites thought only of their own pleasure.

Obviously if it kept their estates going, more power to them. But both Yulan and Violette had been disadvantaged with the arrangement, to put it lightly. All because these idiots couldn't keep it in their pants. Now they wanted to pretend their happiness was pure—that they weren't tarnished by their actions—all the while dumping the stigma on their children?

Sickening.

"That's so...*horrible*...! Why would you say that? You don't know anything about us! You're just biased! I'll have you know, my mother—and my father too, of course—they treat me with so much love—!"

Her impassioned scream was cut short by a shudder. Her big, round, sky-blue eyes had locked with his sunshine gold, only to be scorched by their molten intensity. They weren't merely sparkling—they were incandescent as he stared at her, and the inferno threatened to burn her to ash. He didn't just want her to die; no, he was willing to ensure her death with his own hands. His malice was palpable. Her breath caught and fizzled in her throat.

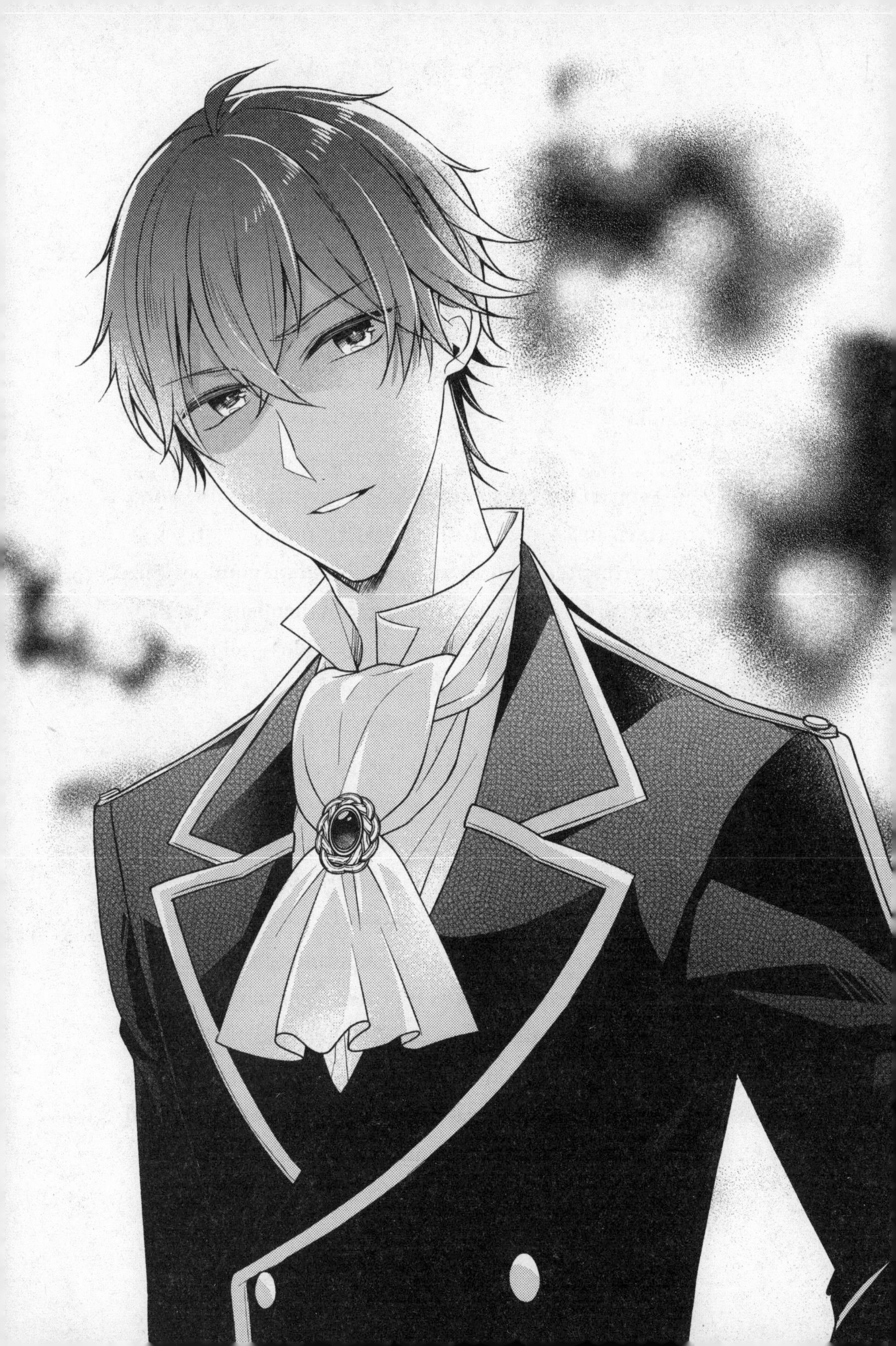

"*Love*, hmm?"

His voice was so soft, one could mistake it for affection—a jarring contrast to his perfectly emotionless face. It was identical to the voice that Maryjune associated with him, yet his expression was steelier than she'd ever seen. It was a showy demonstration of how little she understood him.

"You've honestly never stopped to think about it, have you, you little idiot?"

"Huh...?"

"While you and your parents were a happy little family, where was Violette?"

His voice dripped with open scorn. His contemptuous gaze riddled her with holes. He had no interest in her pain. The little angel was already so pale, she looked to be on the verge of passing out. She could crack her skull open and die for all he cared. Maybe she'd go home and hang herself in despair.

She was so sheltered, her poor little brain couldn't handle what he was telling her without overloading. Spoiled princesses like her grew up thinking that whenever their feelings were hurt, everyone else would come running to help. Well, here was her wake-up call.

"Have you ever paused to imagine, just once, for a single second, where your loving daddy's other daughter was? What her life was like at home with her mother?"

Perhaps now she would realize not everyone lived in luxury. Perhaps now she'd understand who was to blame—and who she'd used as her stepping stone to happiness.

"Surely you're not so stupid as to imagine he could be in two places at once, right?"

With a gasp, she raised a shaking hand to her mouth, her widened eyes brimming with emotion. Now that she could finally, *finally* picture it, it was enough to push her to tears. Had she not had even the slightest inkling until now? She wasn't innocent in that case so much as *brainless*. It was one thing to admire the goodness in someone, but there was a critical difference between ignorance and turning a blind eye to cruelty.

"Uh...I..."

Having learned the truth and sympathized to the point of tears, one could say Maryjune had demonstrated admirable maturity. It was unclear if she regretted her obliviousness, but were she to digest this new information and reflect upon herself without deferring blame, it would indicate her mental fortitude. Now that she knew better, what mattered most was taking action to undo the damage.

Right?

Unfortunately, Yulan didn't care.

"That reminds me. Remember when you said you wanted to be friends with me?"

At this, Maryjune whipped her head up, fearful. As she gazed at him in sorrow, he offered her his most winning smile.

"You ran off before I could answer, so be sure to listen this time."

He crouched down to meet her level. Both pairs of eyes glittered, but for two very different reasons: blue eyes full of tears and terror, and golden eyes filled with acidic contempt. Everything she'd known about him—his friendliness, his smile, his dulcet tones—all of it had fallen away to reveal a face colder than ice and a voice sharper than steel.

"*I'd rather die*, you imbecile."

Yulan poured his poison directly into the little ear peeking out of her pearly white hair.

145 Resolve

LATELY, VIOLETTE felt as though she'd started leaving school earlier than usual... No, she was sure of it. She didn't linger on campus as often as she used to, her study time was markedly shorter than before, and she hadn't spoken to Rosette much, either.

Granted, they were never an inseparable pair of friends to begin with, nor were they each other's only companion; they merely enjoyed each other's company when it was available. When more pressing needs arose, their friendship was put on the back burner. In Violette's case, family was by no means more pressing...and yet...

A sigh escaped her lips. Luckily, no one else was here in her bedroom to hear it. Marin had seen the fatigue etched into her face and stepped away to let her rest. Perhaps she was drawing a lovely bubble bath.

Now that Violette was barred from eating meals in her room, Marin had a little less work to do. Though Violette didn't enjoy her dining hall meals, Marin's presence was the sole silver lining. Nothing good ever came of sitting at that table.

Unlike the intense pressure of eating with Auld, eating with Elfa was a slow suffocation. Being invisible afforded her some measure of peace. But when her every move was being watched under the guise of affection, Violette found herself frozen. Now that supper was over, her muscles were sore from all the tension.

"Mmm..."

Marin had left her with a mug of warm milk, though it was ever so slightly too hot for her sensitive tongue. The warmth of the mug spread to her perpetually icy fingers as she cradled it in her hands. At this time of year, working with water was miserable. Since Marin didn't practice much in the way of self-care, her hands would go painfully red from the cold unless Violette insisted she use some hand lotion.

Gazing into the milk, which rested lower in the cup after a few sips, she reflected on the day's events.

For the first time in an eternity, she'd glimpsed Yulan's smile—but she'd also witnessed panic in him the likes of which she'd never seen before. He had pleaded with her like a boy half his age—not quite *sad*, but threatening tears. He occupied so much of her heart that she scarcely paid attention to her own concerns. It was burned into her thoughts the way he lit up with joy and relief the moment she agreed to...

Right, tomorrow.

Tomorrow they would have a serious discussion over something she "needed to hear." What could it be? Was it a good thing or a bad thing? She wasn't sure, but at that moment, she'd wanted nothing more than to grant his wish, so she agreed to it. Tomorrow, he was going to tell her something important.

Part of her was ever so slightly afraid—not of the details but the discussion itself. She wasn't sure she could bear the weight of his trust if the topic were grave. If it proved too much for her, and she collapsed under it...what then? This could be something truly important to Yulan, and she shuddered to think what might happen if she buckled beneath it.

Still, she couldn't get out of this talk, nor did she want to. No matter how scared she was, it mattered far more to meet Yulan's needs. Even if the details of the discussion were painful for her, if he wanted her to hear it, she would endure it. She was suddenly grateful the topic had been postponed until tomorrow, to give her time to prepare.

But I wonder what's gotten into her...

Maryjune hadn't left her bedroom even once since she got home today, not even for supper, so it was just Elfa and Violette at the dining table. All Violette could remember was Elfa smiling serenely at her while she desperately stuffed food down her throat. She hadn't even had the composure to taste it.

She wasn't informed of any particular reason why Maryjune was absent, but based on what she'd witnessed of her earlier today, it was possible she wasn't feeling well. Perhaps the girl's mental state had in turn impacted her physical well-being. The last time Violette saw her, she *was* looking rather pale.

Violette herself was less concerned about her sister's condition than she was about what the girl might have said to Yulan and whether she was bothering him. *Perhaps I'm heartless.*

Just then, a light knock echoed through the quiet room. *Feeble* was possibly a more accurate description—such a small sound that if Violette had been engaged in conversation, she might not have heard it. Still, it was proof that someone was here to visit.

Marin would have spoken up instead of knocking. Elfa would have knocked much louder.

"Yes...?"

Perplexed, Violette called out, but the visitor didn't enter. Setting her half-full mug on the table, she walked to the door, and after briefly bracing herself, she slowly opened it just enough to peek out.

What she glimpsed was a head of glossy white hair. Feeling every bone in her body scream in protest, she forced herself to open the door wider to reveal a blue-eyed...teenager.

"Maryjune...?"

"My sister...I must speak with you."

Maryjune wasn't wearing her usual sunny smile. No, her expression was more intense than Violette had ever seen. There was no anger to it—only a strong sense of resolve, as though she'd committed her whole heart to something. Only a tiny hint of leftover uncertainty seeped through the cracks.

146 Family Affairs

IT WAS THE FIRST TIME Maryjune had ever visited her bedroom rather than the other way around. Admittedly, she could scarcely remember what Maryjune's room looked like—just that it was packed full of precious memories, and the sight of it had reaffirmed her belief that the two of them would never have anything in common. Back then, she never would have *dreamed* she'd one day allow that same girl into her private quarters. It felt fake even as she watched her.

"If you'd like, I can ask Marin to bring us some refreshments."

"No, that's all right, thank you."

"Very well... Have a seat, I suppose?"

Violette's sofa was dark in color, befitting the overall ambience of the room. Porcelain pale Maryjune looked starkly out of place atop the purple cushions—as though the very furniture was protesting the foreign presence. The only thing these two girls shared was half of their DNA. Nothing more.

Violette sat diagonally across from her on the armchair, but Maryjune remained still as a statue: staring at the floor, biting her lip, her ashen hands clutched in her lap. Violette had never seen this side of her before. All she'd ever really known about Maryjune was her childlike, cheery innocence.

"So...what did you wish to speak with me about?"

"...I always thought of myself as lucky, you know."

In contrast with the statement itself, the girl's voice was frail and brittle, like one might hear inside a church confessional. Her brow was furrowed like she was fighting back tears. Or was she forcing the words out, like bile?

"I have wonderful parents. Whenever I get bullied for the circumstances of my birth, someone's always there to stand up for me. Lots of people care for me, and I care for them just as much, every day of my life. I thought that was normal. Then I learned I had a sister, and we all moved in together. Our family got bigger, and I thought it was such a blessing. Just a normal, good thing."

Maryjune's life was always sunny by careful design. Her mother and father had showered her with love and kindness at every turn, and while she was grateful for it, she never once considered it special. Indeed, she was taught that people ought to be kind and loving and respectful—that it was simply the way of things—and that belief was reinforced over and over by the world around her. She'd taken it for granted that everyone was capable of it. She believed with all her heart that the world was filled with harmony.

"But...what about *your* life, Sister?"

"Maryjune...?"

"When we arrived...when Father was away with us...when you found out you had a younger sister...how did it make you feel?"

Absently, Violette found herself taking note of Maryjune's direct, unwavering eye contact. Her sky-blue eyes shimmered with emotion, but her face was stiff, stubborn, refusing to falter. Behind those ashen lips, she was clenching her teeth.

Violette generally associated her with all things soft and pale, like cotton candy, or marshmallows, or angel feathers. How could someone so pure and innocent have learned the truth? Granted, a little digging would produce plenty of dirt on the Vahan family, but it didn't seem likely that anyone would go out of their way to attack *Maryjune* of all people with it. Did she overhear some gossip? Hopefully she didn't barge into their conversation like with Yulan... The fact that Violette had the mental bandwidth to even contemplate this was proof of how unmoved she was by her sister's emotional display.

Regardless of how, Maryjune had stumbled upon the truth of their family—and her first move was to ask *Violette* about it? Surely she'd know what she was about to hear in response. Had she chosen to confront it head-on?

Well then.

"I wished for death," Violette answered simply.

Maryjune's breath hitched, like she'd taken a blow she knew was coming. Her lip quivered, and her eyes brimmed with emotion... It was obvious she was hurt. Violette also tensed, also felt the tears welling up. In that moment, they had something in common.

She continued, "Death for you, for Father...and for me."

35

I Swear I Won't Bother You AGAIN!

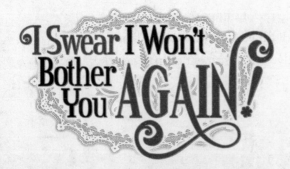

147 Sisters

V IOLETTE'S FEELINGS of hatred and resentment could only be conveyed with strong words like *I'll kill you* or *Go to hell.* It wasn't enough to merely hate them. She'd wanted to inflict on them—on the whole world—the same pain they'd dealt to her.

They weren't the only ones she wished death upon. After all, getting angry and fighting for societal change was nowhere near as easy as simply giving up, lashing out, and taking all the punishment onto herself. *No man is an island,* as the saying went, but life was much, much more peaceful when she put an ocean between herself and the rest of the world.

"I've never once thought of myself as lucky or blessed—or at the very least, I don't associate that feeling with family. I never wanted a family in the first place. I wish you'd all disappear."

Of all the people who brought color into Violette's life, none were blood relatives. Her precious ones dutifully bandaged the wounds inflicted by her so-called "mother," and because of that, she didn't have any (readily visible) scars. It didn't erase the pain, but it meant a lot just knowing someone out there cared enough to patch her up.

She lived her life that way because it was the only option. When her new "family" showed up at her empty house after her mother passed, she wished for a mass death with herself at its epicenter. Only that.

"I will never, *ever* need you people in my life."

At this, the dam burst, and tears spilled from Maryjune's big blue eyes. Much as she tried to fight them, unending streams rolled down the curve of her cheeks. It was heart-wrenching to see her sitting there, crying in total silence, especially when Violette knew she'd been the one to provoke it. But there was something she wanted to test, even if it meant making a little angel weep. She wanted to know how it would feel to see her purehearted sister shed tears on her behalf. She pulled back the curtain, lashed out full force with unveiled malice, and...

Nothing.

I knew it. I'm sorry you're crying your heart out for me, Maryjune...but no matter how hard I try, I'll never be like you.

No thrill, no disappointment, no guilt, nothing. She was as empty as ever. The time for repaying kindness with kindness had long since passed, and she could no longer force herself to care. The gulf between her and Maryjune was simply insurmountable.

She watched absently as her little sister choked back sobs. Sure, she felt *sorry* for Maryjune; it couldn't be easy being related to someone like Violette. Ultimately, she felt no more connection than if the girl were a total stranger. She didn't hate her with the same passion as before—she'd let go of that. Perhaps that was why it all felt so remote.

Those feelings of resentment were a direct reaction to having her hopes betrayed. And oh, what high hopes she'd had for her family— enough to make her *explode* when she was let down. Despite all her rebellion and strife, she still dreamed of being one of them one day... She could no longer remember what that had felt like.

Every one of her hopes had been mercilessly snuffed out until she'd truly lost everything. So when she was given a second chance, she approached it with firm resignation. She would never again hope for love, or trust, or encouragement, or protection, or civility. With this detachment, she was free.

If she would never receive love, then why give it? If she would never be trusted, then why trust? If she would never be supported, shielded, believed, or noticed, then why give these people anything? It was far better for her health not to care. That was how her hatred had died—with all the rest of her emotions. She felt no compulsion to action, be it to give Maryjune a hug or laugh in her face.

"Maryjune...you have no sister."

This family was so utterly incompatible, it was as if an artist had designed it to gracefully fail...and it was falling apart so quickly, no amount of effort was going to save it. They'd had plenty of chances to turn things around—her father, her mother, and Violette included—but they were always going to arrive at this point. It was their destiny as a family.

"Just forget whatever you've heard and move on with your life.

You must accept that sometimes you must cut your losses. There are many things that cannot be healed with kindness alone... Our family is one of them."

Fortunately for Maryjune, this house was the best possible environment for her. A little castle designed to love and protect her. If she could forget about Violette and write it all off as a dream, she could stay in paradise.

Really, it was for the best. Violette would never be any threat to the beloved princess. No matter what she did, she would never get the familial love she'd so violently craved. End of story.

"Sister, I...I...!"

Maryjune slid off the sofa to the floor and clutched at Violette's knees. Either she hadn't fully composed her thoughts or she wasn't sure what to say. Maybe *that* was why she was crying.

There was no telling exactly how much she'd found out, but seeing as she'd come here of all places to talk about it, it must have been enough to shake her trust in her precious parents. Otherwise, she never would have stopped for comfort. No, she'd storm up to the gossipers and give them a piece of her mind. Violette could picture it clear as day.

Maryjune must have come here to learn the truth, and yet... perhaps deep down, she was hoping Violette would say it wasn't true. The sad fact of the world was that people could be kind to one person and cruel to another. Sometimes, "bad" people helped those in need while "good" people stood idly by. This was something hardly anyone understood.

"I'm sorry, Violette...but I...I still love you as my sister!"

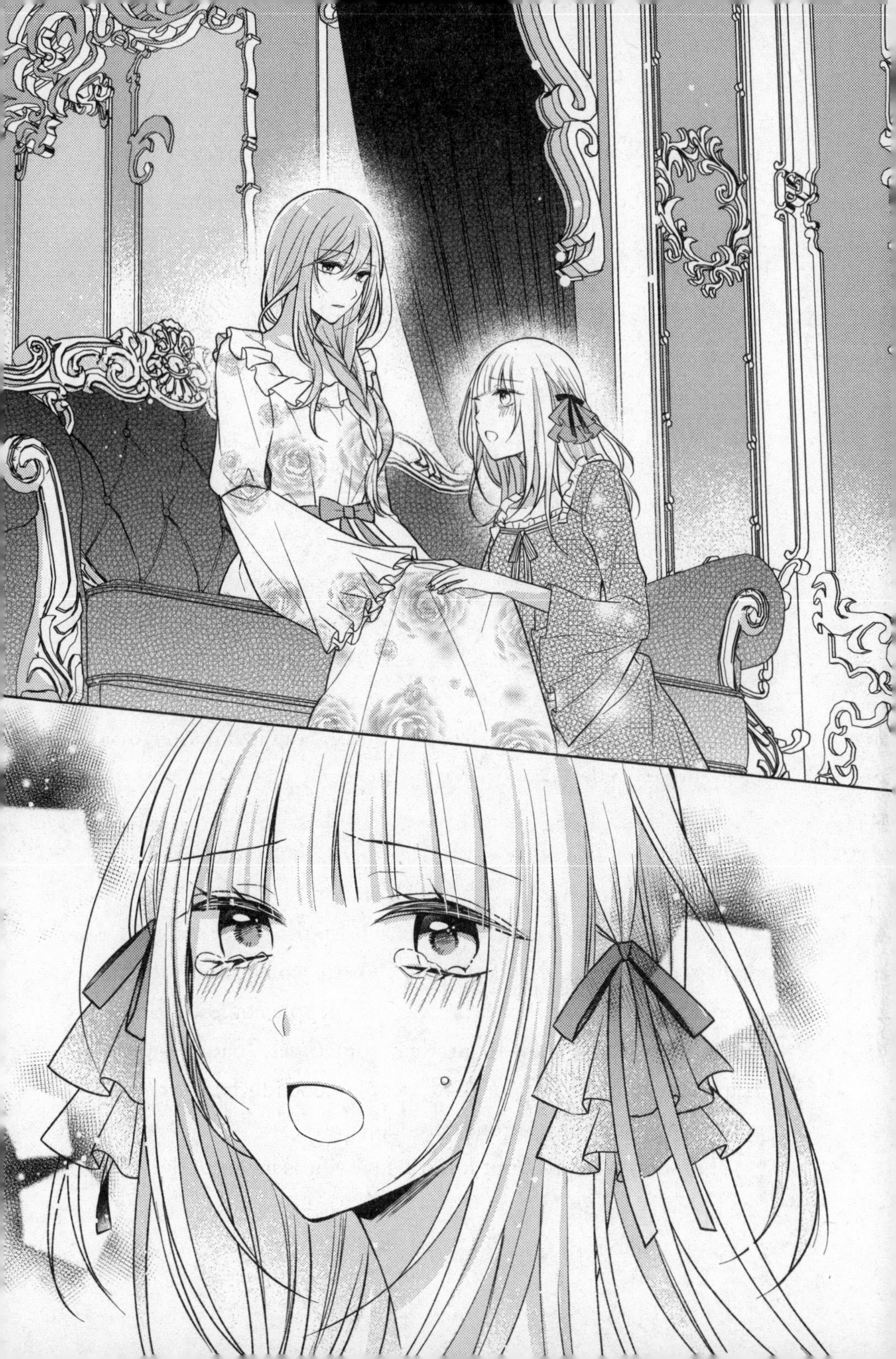

I Swear I Won't Bother You AGAIN!

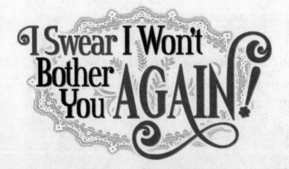

148 Unchanged

IT WAS SAD to see Maryjune crying on the floor. Sweet, really, that she would insist on calling Violette her sister and claim to love her no matter what, but there was a degree of separation to it. It was like seeing a pretty dress through a storefront window— out of reach and quickly forgotten. The notion would evaporate like morning fog and then be gone, soon.

Aww, how lovely...but eh, I don't need it.

"Please, please give me a chance! Just one chance! From now on, I'll think harder about...all of it!"

Her breathing had grown watery, and her speech was slurring. She was already forgetting to choke it back. Tears rolled down her face like pearls and dripped onto the back of her hand as she clutched at Violette's. It was painful to see a pretty girl cry, especially one who smiled so freely.

"I'll give back everything we stole from you! You'll see!"

She grasped Violette's hand as if in prayer, and the top of her head trembled, reminiscent of a child clinging to her mother for consolation. Violette reached out and gave her pearly hair an experimental stroke, but it didn't seem to help. She didn't know what else to do or say.

Precious little angel.

So sweet, so cute, and so very young. Maryjune's eternally childlike spirit was sacred after a fashion, but it was also an indication that she hadn't matured. She only retained this innocent purity because their father hadn't allowed her to develop. She was so sheltered from the slightest hint of danger she'd developed no sense of self-preservation. In her mind, she equated kindness with genuine care, and she believed that "nice" people were nice to everyone without expectation of a return.

The problem wouldn't be solved by *returning what was stolen*. In fact, the concept that it was stolen was pathetically naive. From the outset, this family was built to love only Maryjune. It was impossible to give back that which never existed to begin with.

Violette hadn't realized this in the prior timeline. A second chance at life had allowed her to change as a person, and the world around her changed accordingly. In this timeline she could have a pleasant conversation with Claudia, and she'd even made friends with Rosette. Her toxic posse had stopped coming to see her. Yulan and Marin were still just as nice as before, but they smiled more frequently these days.

The only thing that remained unchanged was her family. No matter how she conducted herself, nothing in this house would ever move. And why would it? She was never a vital cog in this machine. She wasn't needed, so if she was going to stay here, all that was demanded of her was to avoid being a bother.

Back when her mother was alive, being useful was Violette's purpose. She'd served as a stand-in for Auld so that whenever Bellerose lost her temper, it was she who took the brunt of it. The other three lived in harmony in some other house. But now?

Her hand froze on Maryjune's head. It felt as though the obstruction in her mind had finally come loose...as though the very thing she'd been looking for had been right in front of her all this time...as though the missing piece of the puzzle was finally in place—

"Huh...?"

Just then, the muffled sound of shouting drew their attention to the hall outside. Both girls turned to look. Maryjune's eyes were red and puffy, and her cheeks and nose were flushed, like little apples on freshly fallen snow. Before they had time to react, the door flew open with a loud *creak*. A gust of cold air rushed in, either from the hall itself, or...from the icy rage exuding from the intruder.

He glared down at his two daughters nestled close together, his face a thousand times more monstrous than Violette had ever seen it. Maryjune had probably never seen this, either. Her confusion shifted to fear, and she called out in a trembling voice.

"F...Father...?"

I Swear I Won't Bother You AGAIN!

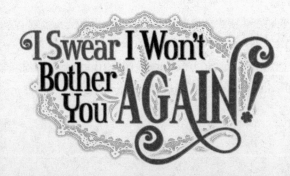

149   Poor Little Lamb

HAD SHE BEEN LIVING in the previous timeline, Violette would have started panicking. With Maryjune crying and her father boiling with rage, it was all too obvious what was about to happen next—so why did she feel so calm? Well, perhaps *calm* wasn't the right word. Her mind was a still lake without the faintest ripple. *Calm* would suggest she had the confidence to handle whatever was thrown at her. Her current state was closer to outright apathy.

Auld stomped over with footsteps as fierce as his expression. Without pause, he reached out and grabbed her by the collar, hauling her up onto her feet. The next thing she knew, her vision pitched sideways. The impact jostled her brain and knocked the sound from her ears. With no time to recover, she hit the floor.

Only then did she realize she'd been struck.

She could just barely make out the sounds of shouting, but her mind was in no shape to process what was said. There were still sparks in her eyes, and her mouth tasted of copper. No chipped teeth as far as she could tell. She must have bitten her cheek.

She put a hand to her face; no swelling yet, but it felt hot to the touch, like a burn. Despite being so monstrous as to hit a woman, evidently her father still had the good sense to strike with an open palm. If only good sense were enough to stop him entirely! He was so enraged, he didn't even seem to notice that she was bleeding. If not for Maryjune fighting desperately to stop him, he probably would have dealt a few more slaps for good measure. He was out of control.

It reminded her of her memories from the previous timeline. With her heart guiding her and her brain checked out, she had felt like a machine on autopilot. Everything felt distant, as if she'd become the very center of the world—as if every societal value hinged on her. She didn't feel the need to reflect on her actions. She was always right, and wrong was whatever she deemed wrong. Past Violette was no different from a beast wearing a human mask.

"It's all *your damn fault*!"

As her hearing returned, her ears picked up every note of resentment and hatred—and the sound of a tiny crack slowly growing larger.

"When will you stop *bothering me*?! How much pain must I endure before you're satisfied?! If it wasn't for you... If only you were never born, I...!"

With every hurled insult, she could hear something breaking. It was her heart, and the walls she'd built around it. She'd tried so hard to turn a blind eye in order to keep living—but now—

"*Stop getting in the way of my happiness!*"

Violette had felt this same feeling—this same venomous hatred. In the previous timeline, she'd taken up a knife with an expression on her face identical to his. There could be no denying it: they shared blood. Originally, she thought she'd inherited it from her mother, but it ran on both sides.

"Stop it, Father! Please!"

"Get out of here, Mary! It's not safe!"

"No, *you* get out of here, Father! Stay away from my sister!"

"What's the matter with you, Mary?! Don't let this vile monster deceive you! She—!"

"Right now, *you're* the vile monster!"

Violette watched as the two of them argued back and forth while she lay there, forgotten. A self-deprecating smile crept up onto her lips; even the stinging pain felt distant. Suddenly everything around her was miles away. She didn't even exist—she was nothing but air. She'd been discarded.

What a pathetic life I've led.

"My lady...?!"

Outside the open door stood Marin, breathing too hard to even speak, like she'd run all the way here at full speed. Though she was doubled over in exhaustion, she still reached out a hand, trying her hardest to call for Violette. It was so sweet, so sad—and that was the moment something inside her finally snapped.

Still on the floor, Violette scrambled right past Auld and Maryjune. The latter called for her to no avail; Violette's legs were tangled in her skirt, but once she started running, it would no longer be a problem. By focusing solely on moving her feet, she could distance herself from the commotion entirely. She had no destination in mind. All she wanted was to go somewhere else—somewhere no eyes or hands or voices could reach her.

"Lady Violette!"

The last thing she heard was Marin's voice, calling out as she struggled to give chase.

DEAR LORD, do you truly despise me this much?

Marin never knew it was possible to feel one's blood boil and run cold at the same time. When she saw Violette on the floor, redness on her cheek and lip, her brain was flooded with despair and rage. After running full speed all the way here, she was out of breath and on the verge of collapsing, but she willed her legs to keep her upright. When that didn't work, she clung weakly to the door frame. She needed to pull Violette into her arms and shield her from the enemy.

Their eyes met. Violette stared back at her dazedly, her emotions unreadable—or had she simply shut down?

Then, before Marin's hand could reach her, she...ran right past.

"Lady Violette—!"

As badly as Marin wanted to chase after the retreating shadow, her legs were shaking too hard to function. She wanted to scream—*Wait! Please! Don't leave me behind!*—but didn't dare say it aloud. Keeping Violette here wouldn't save her now. The second she stopped running, she was as good as dead.

Marin wanted nothing more than to join her getaway scheme, but her legs were agonizingly heavy. Her panicked instinct was to give chase regardless, even if she had to fight not to trip over her own feet. Then, when she saw a certain someone else start to run in the same direction, Marin reflexively grabbed her by the wrist.

"Huh...?!"

"Where do you think *you're* going?"

Though they were both female, Marin was tall and toned from manual labor. She easily overpowered petite little Maryjune. Her unforgiving grip must have been painful, because the younger girl's expression twisted in pain—and the sight of it only added fuel to the flames. There was a murky darkness in Marin's heart that had been left to decay all these years, and now it overflowed. She couldn't remember how it first got there, but it wanted to hurt the person standing before her, and she was rapidly losing control.

"What are you planning to do to her now? What are you going to say? How will you hurt her this time?"

She never dreamed she was capable of wielding her words like a knife. Not that doing it unwittingly made it acceptable, but doing it on purpose was far more cruel. Her rational mind knew hurting people was wrong, but that rationality turned to ash in the flame of rage.

"For once in your life, spare us your arrogance!"

Her vicious glare was enough to make Maryjune flinch. Would she insist she never planned to hurt Violette? Well, Marin didn't care. It didn't matter what Maryjune was planning or how she felt. Her sincerity was worthless.

"We don't need you people."

All these years, which of us was always there to soothe her wounds? Me. Not you. You threw away your right to call yourself her family, and your trash was my treasure. Like hell I'm giving it back now!

As Maryjune began to weep, Marin violently tossed away her grip on the girl's arm; she staggered backward a few steps and sank to the floor. Now, before Daddy Dearest came to check on his little angel, Marin needed to make swift use of her newly regained mobility.

She heard someone shouting from behind her, but she didn't look back.

I Swear I Won't Bother You AGAIN!

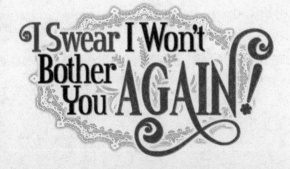

151 Hope, Wish, Dream

MARIN RAN, and ran, and ran across the seemingly endless estate grounds. When she saw the front gates hanging open, the blood drained from her face. Violette hadn't just left the mansion—she'd left the property. She'd flung herself into the cold, dark night with neither a jacket nor shoes.

As the horror of this realization set in, Marin hurtled through the gates...only to stop short as a human figure came into view. For a moment she froze like a startled deer. When she recognized who it was, the tension drained from her shoulders.

"What are you doing here, Chef?"

"Here, eat this."

"Huh...?"

It was Chesuit, leaning against the gatepost with a chocolate cigarette in his mouth. He offered her one as he always did, and she was so caught off guard that she lost all her previous momentum and took it without thinking.

Marin didn't have time for this. The gates were open, so Violette had left the estate grounds. Only the streetlamps could guide her footsteps; the sky was pitch-dark, the moon and stars hidden from sight. It was overcast. It might rain. If Violette was caught out in the rain at this time of year, she'd be risking a lot more than a mild case of the sniffles.

"Sir, I'm in a hurry—"

"If you're worried about the little lady, don't be."

"Do you know where she—?!"

"Go over there and hop in, Mari. Forget about the house. I'll handle it."

He pointed at a glossy black car parked at the curb. It looked a lot like the vehicle that transported Violette to school and back, but Marin suspected this one was different.

"It's cold out here, so wait in there and have him explain the rest."

With no care for her confusion, he crumpled up his chocolate wrapper and stuffed it into his pocket. Then, as she glanced from him to the car and back, he shifted his weight away from the gatepost. She was tall, but he was taller still, and as she craned her neck up at him, she couldn't find any fear in his face. He was acting so normal. It baffled her.

"The young master's with her now."

As someone who had watched over Violette since childhood, Chesuit knew all about her longtime friend. That little boy had always trailed her like a shadow in good times and bad. When everyone else had the good sense to give her space, he alone would refuse to leave her side. Now that little boy had grown up into the man Violette wanted to be with forever.

Neither Chesuit nor Marin could fill those shoes. Violette would never let them see past her smile. Though she was suffering, she would try her hardest to hide it—she'd give up on everything and shrug it off like it was fine. Yulan was the only one who could help her cry.

"All right, I'm heading in. Don't worry about her things. I'll have 'em packed."

Marin's heart was a whirlwind of feelings—of failure, of hope, of uncertainty. The fuse had been lit; there was no going back now. This was the boundary space between heaven and hell, the final branching point, and if they slipped up here, Violette would be tossed to the flames. The mere concept of making a mistake here terrified Marin enough that she yearned for death.

And yet all these fears were swept away by the large hand that ruffled her hair.

"Negotiate with the young master for me, got it?"

"Negotiate...?"

"Convince him to hire me after I get fired for punching my old boss."

He dropped this bombshell so casually, without batting a lash, that she could only blink back at him in stunned silence. In this moment, everything was up in the air, and yet he was already planning for when it landed. He believed that Violette would find happiness.

"...I should negotiate employment for myself as well, I suppose."

None of this situation was reassuring, but she forced herself to smile. It probably looked stiff and fake, but that wasn't important. She'd cast her lot with Chesuit.

Perhaps Violette could have a happy future with Yulan, and Marin could watch over them from afar. Perhaps dreams really *could* come true.

This surge of hope crashed against the wave of fear that pushed her to pursue Violette, and the two feelings battled for dominance. What if Yulan was too late, and Violette gave up on living? The thought brought tears to her eyes, but she was out of options now.

Supposing fear won out and she ran after Violette, there was nothing she could do to save her. She could join her on the path to ruin, but she was powerless to lead her to salvation. Marin had to entrust her hopes in someone else. She didn't need to be the hero. Anything that would give Violette a happy future was justified.

Marin didn't pray...but she was willing to hope firmly. To wish fervently. To dream desperately.

I beg of you, Lord Yulan, please let her cry. Let her scream in pain and acknowledge her misery. Let her vent her resentment of those she despises most. Let her show you her scarred heart at its most vulnerable. Teach her that she's allowed to be sad when she's hurt. After she's gotten every drop out of her system...please...make her smile.

152 Easier Said than Done

Yulan could sleep so much easier if only he had the power of premonition to warn him when his beloved was in danger. Even better, if he could feel everything she felt, then he could come running. Together, their joy was doubled, and their pain was halved—the operative word being "together." Far away, he could do nothing.

So it wasn't her crisis that inspired him to go see her.

After he got home from school, Yulan followed his usual routine, changing out of his uniform and reflecting on the day's events. Nothing he'd said to Maryjune was over the line. He'd gotten a little emotional, but she'd deserved a lot worse. It would have been so much easier if the rumors she overheard had inspired her to start avoiding him instead. Even then, he still would have thrown it all in her face eventually.

His sole concern was her reaction to what he said. Judging from the look on her face when he left, she probably went home and cried. He had sown enough distrust to keep her from seeking help at school, and she didn't have enough fire in her to experience real anger. Best of all, the most dangerous member of the family was currently away from home. Perhaps it was the knowledge of her daddy's absence that had emboldened him.

Other than that, he thought nothing of it—until a maid reported in to his bedroom.

"While you were away, sir, you missed a call from someone by the name of Marin."

Yulan knew at once who it must have been. The name was common enough that there were a handful of fellow students who shared it, but only one face came to mind: striking blue hair and scarlet eyes left an impression, even though they'd barely spoken a word to each other. This woman always stood one step behind Violette, watching vigilantly for any danger, and Yulan respected that about her. She'd never actively sought him out until that fateful day in the previous timeline after all was lost.

His mind jumped straight to the worst possible conclusions, an endless flurry of fuzzy images. When did she call? Today? Yesterday? Before that? Did it have something to do with why Violette seemed so off?

Questions arose in his mind one after another, kindling his panic. His first impulse was anger: *Why didn't you tell me sooner?! If I'd known, I wouldn't have let that self-obsessed ditz cut in line!* Now wasn't the time to shoot the messenger, so he dropped it before it could surface.

"Bring the car around at once. I'm going to the Vahan estate."

Grabbing the nearest jacket, he left the house without entertaining any question or protest from the servants.

Inside the car, no one spoke a word. Closing his eyes, Yulan swayed with the faint vibrations as he willed himself to stay calm. Pessimism was a fog that clouded his rational mind. If he swung an axe at the shadow of a bear only to discover it was human, there would be no repairing the damage. He couldn't let his perception be warped by negative assumptions.

He was merely going to check on her. If nothing was wrong, then he wouldn't risk kicking the hornets' nest; he'd go home and wait patiently for tomorrow. Yes, hopefully he was overreacting. Hopefully it was just paranoia. He would be happy to know he'd wasted his time if it meant she was unharmed—

"Stop the car!"

By pure chance, he'd glanced out at the brick streets illuminated by streetlamps—and there, in the darkness, was a flash of trailing gray that disappeared a split second after he glimpsed it.

When the car pulled over, he jumped out. He was only wearing a thin cardigan over his undershirt, and it wasn't enough to fend off the biting cold. The warmth was already draining from his ears and fingertips. He knew what he'd seen.

"Vio!"

She'd already vanished into the night. There was no chance she'd hear him. His mind was too consumed to process any of that. His plan had just been thrown out the window, and he didn't know what to do. A rational thinker would have known to give chase above all else, but he was too hung up on trying to figure out why she was here in the first place.

"Young master?"

Out on the deserted street, the sudden voice made him turn. He hadn't assumed he was the one being addressed, but sure enough, the speaker was looking straight at him.

The man was around the same height as him, yet he seemed much larger. His broad chest, thick biceps, muscular hands—all signified a powerful masculinity. Unlike Yulan, whose boyish features gave off a harmless air, this was a man's man. Though he was wheezing and sweating like a marathon runner, he was dressed in chef's whites. Yulan noticed the fraying, slicked-back brown hair and jade green eyes and realized he recognized the man's face.

"You're...the Vahan estate's..."

Amid dizzying panic, Yulan struggled to remember, but Chesuit calmly cut it short.

"Yes, but let's skip introductions. Neither of us have the time."

Chesuit surveyed him with an expression that betrayed no hostility or emotion of any kind. His gaze was oppressive. His physical attributes were intimidating, admittedly, but that wasn't what gave Yulan pause. Rather, the man looked through him like glass, observing his flustered confusion. This was a grown man, and Yulan was just a boy.

"The master of the house returned ahead of schedule," Chesuit explained, and when Yulan's breath hitched, he continued, "I take it you can guess what happened."

Out here in the chilly night air, Yulan was suddenly aware of the wetness trickling down his back. The unpleasant cold sweat lingered while his blood—no, even his *breath*—drained away. He suddenly couldn't get any oxygen, and his shallow respiration tightened the vise on his heart.

Had he failed all over again?

Crack!

Just then, there was a loud, sharp sound, like the popping of a balloon, clearing his mind.

"Pull yourself together, kid. It's too early to throw in the towel."

Two hands were pressed together before his eyes. Yulan realized Chesuit must have clapped to get his attention. The man's palms were bright red from the cold.

Just like that, his tumbling, snowballing thoughts were forced to a halt. Not a moment too soon—otherwise he might have fallen apart inside, dragged to rock bottom by his own self-sabotage. At that point, what followed would be little more than a repeat of that fateful day at the church. He already knew no amount of crying before God would ever save her. Hadn't he promised himself he'd never give up?

"...Right, sorry. I'll go to her."

"Know where she is?"

"I have a few...educated guesses."

"Then I'll let you handle it. I've got a second one to worry about."

Yulan could already imagine who he was referring to—Marin, whose firsthand knowledge of Violette's pain meant she was always prepared to throw herself into the line of fire. If Violette had run out of the Vahan mansion, then Marin would give chase without question. Hell, she'd spend all night searching the city if she had to, her own health be damned.

"I'll have my driver give you a lift. There's somewhere I'd like Miss Marin to go."

He offered Chesuit and his driver a condensed explanation with their instructions, then slammed the car doors shut. No time to lose. He didn't even wait for them to drive away before he took off running in the opposite direction. They had been given the bare minimum—they knew what to do once Marin was evacuated. Now Yulan just needed to find Violette.

Though he did have a few "educated guesses," as he'd put it, there was no guarantee they'd lead him to her. Her destination could be elsewhere entirely, or perhaps she was wandering aimlessly; he had no concrete evidence. And yet...for some reason, he was sure he would find her.

No matter where she went, no matter what it took, even if he had to lower himself to the earth and crawl like a worm, he didn't care. He'd already seen the depths of hell. He had clenched his teeth in boiling rage at the beauty of the light that refused to shine on his beloved. He'd vowed to defy it and give her a happy future. He carried all these feelings with him. He'd decided— whether motivated by anger, hatred, or joy—he would never give anything up. Ever.

153   Let's Go Home

ONE BY ONE, Yulan ran through each of the places they had visited together. Then he went down the list of every place Violette had mentioned to him offhand. He retraced their shared memories.

One place they'd visited in middle school. Another from when they graduated elementary school. A store they could only see through the window. He remembered being devastated when they were told children weren't permitted inside.

They made trips to the library and the botanical garden—anywhere to get her away from her parents. Little moments here and there that composed their shared history. There was another special place out behind the Vahan estate at the end of a narrow trail deep into the woods.

Decaying birdhouses and gnarled old trees. Right, left, left, right. There, one would find a small clearing blanketed with flowers, or weeds, or something in between. A far prettier sight than the slimy moss and termite-damaged trees, though it was still dirty with mud and dead leaves. There, in the center, was a small, feeble figure, sitting like a discarded doll with her head slumped against her knees.

"Man, this place takes me back."

He called out to her as he approached, but she didn't stir. No reaction, though he doubted she could have predicted his arrival. He wasn't expecting to find himself back here, let alone under these circumstances. The trees had seemed so tall back then, and the clearing so wide, but now it all looked a lot smaller. Too small, perhaps, for a pair who had left their childhoods behind.

Those were the days when they didn't get in trouble for holding hands...and back then, this place was their true home.

It was just a flower field. In winter there wasn't much but mud and weeds. No one was tasked with its maintenance, so it was falling apart. When they came here, all they could do was sit and draw pictures in the dirt with sticks. But a home was a safe, happy place where you could be with your loved ones—and that was what this was.

This was no tree fort or playground; they weren't supposed to come here, but the mansion was too miserable and scary to be a home. She may have slept at the mansion, but *this* was the place she longed to return to. They agreed they always would.

Of course. This was the farthest a little girl could reasonably escape. She belonged in the forest, not that awful Vahan estate. She desperately convinced herself she had another home she could flee to so she could find the strength to keep living.

"How long's it been since our last visit? It gets dark awful quick in these woods, so we kinda stopped coming by once school started."

He knelt beside her, the chill of the wet earth seeping through his slacks. Slowly, the cold filtered in through the fabric. While he was grateful for the absence of sharp stones under his knees, the mud was undeniably draining his body heat.

"Aren't you cold, Vio? Best I've got is this little cardigan. It might not help much."

He pulled it off and laid it over her shoulders, knowing how ineffective it would be. Surely it had to be better than nothing. His fingers brushed against her ice-cold hair, and it was painfully apparent just how long she'd been there.

Only then did Violette finally raise her head. Her bangs fell over her face in a curtain, and her eyes wandered, empty and unfocused, like two inert marbles. What drew his attention most of all was the bright red mark running from her cheekbone to her jaw. Over time, it would surely swell up even larger. More frightening still, there was blood—dried, thankfully—at the corner of her mouth, suggesting there was a cut somewhere inside. She'd been struck with considerable force.

"Vio...you...?"

"Yulan."

His trembling lips struggled to form words. It wasn't until after he called her name that he recognized the throbbing sound in his ears as his own quickening pulse. He knew the slightest touch would likely hurt, and yet he reached out all the same, desperate to heal her with his own two hands. If only he could physically pluck the pain away.

"Huh...?"

Just then, as his fingers wavered in their approach, Violette laid her hand on his and guided it to her injury. He tried to pull back on sheer reflex, but her grip was surprisingly firm as she kept him pinned there. In contrast to his cold hand, the swell throbbed with heat, just as he'd imagined from its color.

"Yulan."

Her voice was flat and lifeless—no edge, but a blade to his heart all the same. From her empty eyes, a droplet trickled down the back of her hand, followed by a second, then a third, until a stream had formed. She wept, calling his name over and over like a broken toy. Then, as he struggled to breathe, a muffled sound reached his ears—tiny and hoarse, yet clear: "I don't want to live anymore."

154 Be with Me Forever

VIOLETTE HADN'T WANTED to bother anyone. If she couldn't be of use, then she at least wanted to avoid being a hindrance. She thought if only she stayed out of the way, they'd tolerate her. She could live with being unneeded as long as she wasn't discarded.

She wanted someone—anyone—to accept her, even if only begrudgingly. They never would. After all, her very existence was an obstacle.

She didn't want to die; she was as apathetic about death as she was about life. She couldn't see the value in it. She was just *tired*. Tired of hurting, tired of suffering, and even if it was a burden she was meant to carry as penance for her crime, she was tired of living.

All she wanted was permission to exist, the same as everyone else. She thought she was entitled to that much, at least. She was wrong. Her wish couldn't come true.

That was that.

I don't care anymore. It doesn't matter. I'm so sorry, Yulan— I know you wanted to have an important discussion, and I'm sure you're worried about me, but...

Wait, how did you know I was here? How did you know I ran away from home? And...why are you crying?

"...Yulan?"

A single teardrop descended from his golden eye like honey from a jar. There was no grimace of pain or misery, only a muted expression as he sank into grief. At some point his hand had fallen away from her face, and now it dangled limply to the ground.

This time it was her turn to reach out to his face, sliding her thumb under his eye to stop the tear in its tracks. The tiny drop of moisture had a spreading warmth to it. As if mimicking her gesture from earlier, he laid his hand on hers. Gently, he pulled her against his broad chest, where his faint heartbeat thrummed in her ears. His strong arms held her tight, preventing the slightest shift, even constricting her breath.

"Let's get married."

His voice poured into her heart like an element of nature— like the rustle of leaves in the wind, or the patter of rain, or the river joining the sea.

"We'll eat delicious food, travel to all sorts of places, and rest when we're tired. We'll share a laugh, share a bed... We'll sleep together, wake together, make small talk about the weather... Everything you want to own, to get rid of, to do, to get out of— I'll make it all happen for you."

Every word was a shining star—something she'd always thought beyond her reach. They showered down onto her in such great numbers, she couldn't possibly carry them all with both hands. Not even in both arms.

"Be with me forever. Let me stay with you, and don't leave me behind. Always remember that I'm on your side."

These words echoed a time when she'd asked what she could do for him; in response, he'd only wished to share her space. This time, the sentiment was expressed with more passion than ever, wrapping her up in its warmth and gentle rigidity. It was so sweet, but she was frightened too... Emotions she thought she'd long since lost were now blooming inside her, one after another.

"Give this a try with me, and if you still don't want to live... then take me with you."

The next thing she knew, his tears had dried. Her cheeks must have felt so strange against his palms, with some parts freezing cold from the winter air and others, like the welt on her face, burning hot. His gaze, his smile—both struck right at her core, slowly wedging her open from the inside.

Her skirt was wet and cold, and the toes inside her slippers were like chips of ice. Her lips and cheeks felt funny, and the scrapes she'd gotten on the run here were tingling faintly. She was cold and hurt and suffocating...and happy.

I guess I'm still alive.

"...You mean it?"

"Yeah."

"You'll come with me?"

"Yeah."

If a day like today ever happened again, and she was in so much misery that she couldn't bear the thought of enduring another day... If ever she chose to give up hope and throw it all down the drain...

"You'll really...die with me?"

You'll be with me forever?

"Yeah."

He nodded without missing a beat, wearing a dreamy smile as though it was the happiest moment of his life. She sensed he would smile for her like that on the day they decided to end it all. It was how Yulan was, how he would always be.

Violette's nose stung, and her expression crumpled. Did she want to laugh or cry? Both, probably. She didn't know what she was supposed to say, but perhaps she didn't truly *need* to say anything. Instead, she simply followed her heart—and flung her arms around his neck.

There was still so much to be afraid of. Not even the most beautiful words were capable of instantly bringing back her numbed emotions and everything else she'd abandoned. Perhaps she would give up completely before they ever had the chance to return; it was a far more appealing prospect than to reach out only to be smacked down. Whether she let go or held fast, either way, it no longer mattered.

Yulan had promised to be with her in life and death. With him at her side, she had nothing to fear.

155 After a Good Cry

T HEY COULD EMBRACE each other all they liked, but with no insulating coats, they were rapidly losing body heat. Violette in particular had raced out of the house in her loungewear and spent an indeterminate amount of time curled up out here in the forest. No measly cardigan would mitigate that.

Her knees and bottom were muddy from sitting on the ground, and her slippers were so utterly soaked that she was arguably better off not wearing them. Her pale skin was flushed painfully red from the cold; paired against the thin fabric of her dress, it was pitiful upon pitiful. Yulan needed to get her someplace warmer fast, or else she'd be at risk of a lot more than a runny nose.

"Sorry about this, Vio."

"Huh...?"

With her arms already around his neck, Yulan wrapped his own arms around her waist and knees and lifted her up. The sudden floating sensation startled her, and instinctively she clung to him...but when their eyes met and they were nose to nose, he could tell from her flustered expression that her ears hadn't turned red because of the cold.

This position was often called a bridal carry, but it felt less like an act of seduction and more like a rescue operation. While he didn't know Violette's exact weight and had never carried her like this before, Yulan got the sense that she was much lighter than she used to be. This close, her face seemed gaunt... He could only curse the days he'd spent away from her.

"It's not safe for you to put weight on those feet. Hang tight until I get you to the car, okay?"

"I'm sorry..."

"Don't be, silly. Not to make light of this, but I'm pleased."

"Pleased?" she repeated.

"Yeah. I've gotten strong enough to carry you."

"...Unlike last time, when you dropped me."

"God, you remember that?"

"It took *ages* to nurse your bruised ego."

Back then, he'd been insistent that he could protect her. In truth, he hadn't had enough strength to so much as lift her. He cried like a baby, and his dainty damsel had to console him... The memory was so shameful, he almost wanted to cry all over again.

He'd never enjoyed exercise, but from that point forward, he vowed to start training his body. He was now bigger than he ever imagined he could get, but he likely owed it more to genetics than dedication. Still, he'd gotten stronger in more ways than one. He wouldn't complain.

"Do me a kindness and erase that from your memory, would you? You're the only person who's ever seen me cry, you know."

That one incident aside, he had never cried as a child. Not even when he took a beating. Once he learned how to hold a poker face, he would simply grimace. Gia called him an unfeeling monster because of it. Yulan was inclined to agree.

Deep down, he was a defective human—or perhaps *broken* was the better word. All sorts of people had broken him in all sorts of ways. He only retained a humanoid shape because Violette had worked so hard to piece him back together again. Everything he did was in service to her alone, and that included his tears.

"The same goes for me as well. I've only cried in front of you and...Marin, I suppose."

Like Yulan, Violette's psyche had been stabbed full of holes by various assailants with any number of weapons. The only difference between them was apathy versus resignation. In contrast to Yulan, who had stopped caring about anything long ago, Violette still believed in *family* and *love* and other such concepts. That was why she'd clung to them for dear life in the previous timeline. She may not have been purehearted, but she was tenderhearted to a fault.

He could only imagine how much it must have hurt—not just physically but emotionally. Not just today, either. She'd suffered miserably her whole life. She must have felt so alone, being unable to weep over it.

"I always get hungry after a good cry, don't you? After we get there, I'll order you a delicious dessert."

"That sounds nice... Wait, get *where*?"

"Hmm?"

"Erm...aren't we...returning to the estate?"

"What, did you need to go back and grab something? I'll pick it up for you later. Or I can send someone."

"That's not what I..." Her eyes wavered in uncertainty, still damp from tears. The confusion made it easy for her to panic.

She'd assumed he was delivering her back to hell. Now that she'd regained her composure, she felt she had no choice but to go back and beg for forgiveness. While it was the path of least resistance, Yulan would *never* permit it.

"I want to take you somewhere, Vio."

"But...I..."

"It's going to be okay. Please?"

She hung her head in pained silence for a moment, then nodded slightly. If he had to guess what could be holding her back, it was the special someone she'd left behind. The reason she didn't try to escape was because her hunger for family kept her magnetized to Marin. The two young women were fully reliant upon each other for love and support, and as a result, they were inadvertently holding each other hostage. It was something they'd need to hash out together in private, going forward.

As Yulan waited for the car to find them, he felt Violette's slender fingertips clutch anxiously at his collar.

156 Boundary Line

BUNDLED UP in big, fluffy towels, they swayed as the car carried them to a luxury hotel. Its match in opulence could only be found in a handful of other hotels in the country. Foreign dignitaries may have found the level of security lacking, but in all other regards, its service was of the highest quality.

In a perfect world, Yulan would have had a household ready instead, but that wasn't something he could arrange in a matter of hours. The fact that he'd acquired the hotel reservation on such short notice was miracle enough. Tomorrow he would ask Violette for her thoughts and reserve a different, more expensive room for her if needed.

"Yulan, I—"

"How are your injuries?"

"Oh, um...f-fine..."

"Glad to hear it. Your room's right next to the elevator, so hang in there a little longer, okay?"

He knew from experience how effective his smile would be in easing her confusion. Her injuries were genuinely concerning to him, but in a few minutes he would hand her over to someone who was far more capable of patching her up.

When they arrived at their floor, their destination was the very first door. Violette's eyes quavered in uncertainty as she looked up at him, but thanks to the years of trust they had established, she showed no signs of fear. This was an uncommon bond coming from such a deeply guarded girl, although no amount of trust could truly erase her confusion at these unpredictable circumstances. That, too, was a certain someone else's job.

"Okay, Vio, hold out your hand."

He pressed the newly acquired key into her slender palm, already much warmer than it had felt outside. Her gaze flitted down and then back to Yulan, perplexed.

"This is as far as I go. There should be clean clothes and other things waiting for you inside, but if there's anything else you need, you can contact me anytime. And there's twenty-four-hour room service, so be sure to eat whenever you feel hungry."

That was the moment fear finally crept over her—the fear of Yulan leaving. Generally speaking, it wasn't proper for a lady to ask a gentleman to stay the night with her at a hotel; Yulan himself was no threat to her, but still...he wasn't sure if her lack of apprehension was a sign of trust or of total disinterest in him as a member of the opposite sex. Either way, he would leave. This was the boundary line.

"Sweet dreams. I'll see you tomorrow."

He planted a kiss on the crown of her little head and felt the chill of her hair against his lips.

Violette could only watch as Yulan walked away, wearing that soft, sweet smile of his right to the last moment. She knew she couldn't ask him to stay; after the lengths he'd already gone to, it would be wrong of her to expect more. Love had given her so much already, but that didn't mean *carte blanche* was part of the deal.

In the absence of his warmth, the key in her palm suddenly felt so cold...or did she simply feel guilty about the service to which it entitled her?

I wonder what's happening back at the house...

If she'd stayed a moment longer, she was certain she would have died—and if it was going to happen either way, then she at least wanted it to be on her own terms. Thus her feet had carried her out of the house, spurred by raw emotion.

She wasn't worried about the estate, and she suspected the apathy was mutual. The cogs would keep on turning whether she was absent for a night or the rest of her life. Perhaps Maryjune would feel some semblance of pain, but Violette didn't care. In the past, maybe, but that was over.

No, what concerned her about the house was the irreplaceable treasure she'd left behind. The poor woman was surely worried sick about her, perhaps even crying herself to sleep that very moment. It must have broken her heart to be abandoned like that. She might even have been punished for letting Violette escape.

So why was it, then, that this sole regret...

"Lady Violette!"

...was waiting for her in the room?

157 The Southern Star Blooms

THE MOMENT she opened the door, Violette was engulfed by a flash of sky blue and just enough warmth to indicate a living being. A pair of arms wrapped around her head, and the racing heartbeat against her ear was enough to convey just how frightened its owner had been for her.

"Thank goodness! Truly...what a relief...!"

It pained her to hear Marin's voice so hoarse and watery. The woman's fingers and palms traced through Violette's hair and along her silhouette, again and again, as if to make doubly, *triply* sure she was really there. The arms around her tightened, refusing to let her go, enough to make her suffocate—not from hostility but from love and gratitude.

"I'm sorry... I'm...so sorry...!"

"It's all right, my lady. Everything's all right now."

"I'm sorry! So...sorry...!"

"It's okay now. It's okay."

The warmth brought the pain back into focus—her cheek, her lips, her hands, her feet. What hurt Violette most of all was the thought that she'd scared Marin. All she could do was return the embrace and apologize through her tears. Add in the dried blood and swelling, and her face was a total mess.

There was so much she wanted to ask. What was Marin doing here? What about the estate? Had Violette's actions cost Marin her job? It felt like her heart was back in the vise's grip. The mere thought of harming Marin filled her guts with smoldering lead.

She wanted to talk about it, but the words wouldn't come. Her brain wasn't working. All she could say was *I'm sorry*, and she felt so pathetic, she couldn't stop crying...but it meant so much to feel that reassuring hand at her back. The two of them clung to each other, wailing like children, until at last their energies and tears were spent.

There was much to discuss, but first came a hot meal, then a bath, and then first aid... They continued to delay their heart-to-heart until Violette felt the urge to doze off, and in a blink, she was sound asleep. She was exhausted, yes, but more than that, she was finally free from that house. In recent days she'd spent many a night tossing and turning, so for tonight, perhaps she was relieved to no longer share a roof with the enemy. Stranger that her own bed was *less* comforting than a strange place, luxury hotel or otherwise.

Violette had fallen asleep face-first on the bedspread, her

head never reaching the pillow. Though her posture looked uncomfortable, her expression was deeply peaceful.

Marin retrieved a spare blanket, laid it over her mistress, and watched as she curled into a ball beneath it. When she rolled over, the large bandage on her cheek came into view. Likewise, her loosely clenched fingers and concealed feet were colored unnaturally white from the gauze.

I should have decked him before I left.

At the time, Marin's only thought was of chasing after Violette, but if she was going to leave the estate regardless, then she ought to have landed a few blows for good measure. Hindsight was twenty-twenty. She had no way of knowing then that Yulan was already tracking Violette down. Still, looking back uncovered dozens of similar half regrets she couldn't begin to forgive...and so her hatred of the culprit steadily grew.

After she climbed into the car as instructed by Chesuit, she was greeted by the Cugurs family chauffeur, who directly drove her to this hotel. Then he got back into his car and drove off, leaving her countless questions unanswered. Even now, she still didn't quite understand what was going on. All she had to go on was the hope offered by Yulan's message, passed on to her by the chauffeur: *Wait here for Violette.*

Trusting in those words, she occupied herself by arranging the room for Violette's convenience—otherwise, the anxiety might have driven her to fling herself wholly into the arms of despair. Every second felt like an eternity as she prayed to a worthless god for her beloved to return. *Please, please let Violette be alive.*

In the end, sure enough, Yulan brought her just as he'd promised, and thanks to him, Marin had felt her living, breathing warmth once more.

"Welcome home, Lady Violette."

Perched on the edge of the spacious bed, she ran her fingers through Violette's silvery hair. It glittered in the low light, as soft as its owner's heart. That texture wasn't always silky; some days, it could turn brittle without enough moisture and care, leading to breakage. Violette's true beauty was beyond compare, but rarely was it nurtured enough to reach its full potential.

"From now on, it's going to be okay."

Yes, Marin had faith that it would be. She didn't know *how*, or *why*, or even what "it" was—nothing was guaranteed—but there was nothing left to fear with Violette at her side. Yulan's chosen strategy was a mystery, but he had the power to rescue Violette. Marin would obey his orders. What she wanted more than anything was the means to protect her mistress, and she'd long since prepared to gladly submit herself to be his pawn or whatever else he demanded of her.

I only pray Chef Chesuit is all right...

Her one lingering concern was centered on the man burdened with cleaning up their mess. Perhaps it was unwarranted. Chesuit was far older and more experienced than she was. With Violette gone, however, the estate was sure to be in an uproar for all the wrong reasons—and there were overwhelmingly few people capable of reining it in properly.

By Marin's estimate, only Chesuit could defy the master of the house without hesitation. He had the superior brain and brawn, but when it came to matters of employment, the boss always came out on top. Still, Chesuit was a man of his word...

I hope he didn't punch that man.

She did enjoy imagining it. That monster deserved to be struck with the full force of a grown man—hard enough to remodel his face. Was it worth the punishment Chesuit would inevitably suffer? No, sadly.

"Tomorrow..."

Everything hinged on tomorrow. Something would be set in stone—something would end, and something else would begin. Knowing it would all determine Violette's future, she prayed: *When your soft snores end, and you wake in the morning light...may your eyes only find happiness.*

I Swear I Won't Bother You AGAIN!

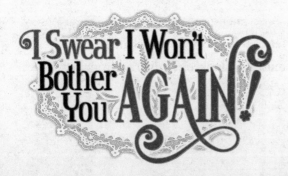

158 Comet Orchid

The next thing Violette knew, it was morning. The last thing she remembered was opening the door to find Marin... She must have been so relieved that she passed out.

Normally she was the type who struggled to fall asleep and rarely ever dreamed. She fell into darkness only to snap suddenly awake. This time, however, in the moments after she woke, she simply lay there, staring into space. Like yesterday, the world felt weightless and fuzzy.

"Lady Violette, would you like to get some more rest?"

"Oh, I'm all right. Thank you."

"You say that, but you appear to be eating spoonfuls of *air*."

"Huh?"

At this, she looked down to find that her bowl of soup was untouched. That would explain why she thought it tasted bland and flavorless: evidently, she'd been putting the spoon in her mouth entirely empty. Her cheeks flushed with shame as she imagined how stupid she must have looked. To distract from her faux pas, she carefully filled her golden spoon with golden broth as she'd originally intended.

Though it was steaming faintly, soup prepared by Marin was never too hot to eat. Ignoring the feel of the other woman's eyes intently observing her, she slid the spoon into her mouth. Sure enough, the heat of the consommé wasn't strong enough to burn her tongue. It was a bit thicker than she was used to but delicious all the same. Still, her favorite would always be Chesuit's home-made soup, packed full of tender veggies.

Now that she'd escaped the Vahan estate and Marin was here with her, she'd thought she'd never look back, but…it was a little disappointing—no, more than a little—that she'd never get to eat his cooking again.

"…Marin?"

"What is it, my lady?"

"What happened at the house?"

Marin stayed silent.

"You were my only personal maid, and since I made an effort to distance myself from the rest, I'm sure they're all fine…but…"

There were two categories of servant at the house: those who had served since Violette's mother Bellerose was alive and those who were hired to serve the happy family of three. All the latter and most of the former were complicit in Violette's mistreatment, but there were still quite a few who worried for her. Chief among them was Marin, followed by the head chef Chesuit.

When Bellerose was alive, anyone who tried to protect Violette would only make things worse. Most of them were fired for trying. Those who were left gritted their teeth and endured the abuse in order to stay in Violette's life. When the lady of the house passed and the nightmare was over, the master showed up with his new family, tripling the burden overnight.

Marin found this immensely frustrating. Though they supplied her income, she loathed her employers intensely—and yet, despite all her righteous indignation, she knew she must endure. Not even she was allowed to act as Violette's sword or shield if she wanted to stay by the girl's side.

Supposing she *had* leapt to Violette's defense and lost her job as a result. What would happen after that? What would become of her poor mistress? She would be screamed at, insulted, used as a punching bag until it broke her—and eventually killed. The implied threat of this kept everyone's hands tied.

Whether she realized this or not, Violette herself started keeping her distance from all the staff, save for Marin, to avoid any more needless firings. She never spoke to any of them more than strictly necessary, and only after ensuring that no one was watching. Fortunately—well, as much as *fortune* could be applied to such a situation—this meant there was no one at the house her father could blame for her escape. Conversely, if they'd had the opportunity to be kind to her or serve her in any way, it would have painted a target on their backs.

"If you'd still been there, I would have gone back for you."

"If I were still there, I would have set fire to the whole manor with all three of them trapped inside so you'd never set foot inside again."

"What...?!"

This remark was so alarming, Violette immediately looked up—only to be alarmed even more by Marin's expression. The woman's sunset-hued eyes were narrowed, her lips curved in a perfect arc, her short hair flowing like water to one side as she tilted her head. Her features were cold and beautiful, reminiscent of an ice sculpture...yet she wore the soft, gentle smile of a saint. She was the Holy Mother given flesh.

"You no longer have anywhere to return, Lady Violette. No obligation binds you. From now on, you will travel only where you wish to go. *You* decide where home is."

She knelt and took Violette's hand in both of hers, stroking it firmly yet lovingly, like she was massaging the new reality into her very bones.

"I will be with you, always. I will go with you wherever you so choose."

Oh, how long Marin had waited for the day she could say these very words.

"You needn't be afraid any longer."

159 Let's Talk of Dreams

DEEP IN HER HEART, Violette felt the missing piece of the puzzle finally click into place. It wasn't a fulfilling feeling but rather the relief of finding the one thing she'd never had. Though she'd always known what the completed puzzle would look like, she needed the final fragment to piece it all together in a way that made sense.

The last chain holding her down was *fear*.

This came as no surprise. To a child, even the most monstrous parental figure was akin to a god. The parent-child link was a persistent one. It wasn't difficult for those without exceptional power to dominate the weak nevertheless, and this was all the truer if the target of subjugation was one's own spawn.

The most reliable way to defeat fear was to escape, but it was also the hardest. After all, someone could distance themselves from the source of it, but they could never escape that which was embedded deep in the heart.

She's right... It's over.

It didn't move her to tears. She absorbed the information as the fact it was—simple and unspeakably freeing.

❧

"Morning! Did you sleep well?"

"Good morning, Yulan."

After breakfast came a pleasant spot of tea, followed by the arrival of Yulan, who entered the room at Marin's behest carrying a paper bag. His smile and voice were the same as always—so natural and reassuring, Violette could *almost* be convinced that the events of last night were all a dream.

When his gaze landed on her bandaged cheek, for the briefest of moments, relief and anger flashed in his eyes. By the time he sat down next to her, it was gone.

"If the pillows weren't to your liking, I was prepared to reserve a better room somewhere else," he continued, "but it seems that won't be necessary."

"Not at all. The bed was so comfortable, I completely overslept," she replied.

"Heh! Glad to hear it. If there's anything else you need, say the word and I'll have it delivered."

"Thank you, but I'm fine. You've already done more than enough for me."

"Your idea of 'enough' is almost *never* actually enough, Vio."

"Then *I* shall utilize my best judgment and report to you, if necessary," Marin cut in casually as she brought a third cup to the table.

"Perfect," Yulan nodded.

The two had only ever interacted through Violette, yet here they were, chatting like old friends. It was a peculiar sight. But Violette was hardly bothered; if anything, she was delighted that her two favorite people were on good terms with one another.

"Oh yeah, I was told to bring this for you two."

Once Marin was present, Yulan lifted the paper bag from the floor and set it on the table. Only then did Violette realize just how large it was. The ease with which he carried it had made her think it wasn't filled with much. Judging from the way he was reclining, cup in hand, the ball was now in their court. So she and Marin peered inside together.

The interior was neatly arranged, each item bundled to avoid damaging the others. At first glance it was hard to tell precisely what was inside. As they proceeded to pull it all out, her first thought was proven correct—nothing too heavy. Just little things or large yet lightweight things. By the time they'd finished emptying the bag, the table was half covered in white paper.

"Are these...?"

As they unwrapped each one, however, it quickly became apparent exactly who this delivery was from.

The larger parcels were items of clothing: two of Violette's favorite pieces, hand-selected from her entire massive wardrobe, and a few of Marin's aprons and plain clothes. The smaller parcels were their beloved old tools, dishware, and accessories—things they would have sorely regretted leaving to rot in that house.

Hair clips received as a gift, the pocket watch Marin had picked out for Violette, the mug used for her warm milk, the hand lotion Violette had given to Marin, the princess storybook they read in secret when Bellerose was asleep, the planner in which Marin had recorded her mistress's behavior... Each was a precious memento they had squirreled away—treasures that would surely have been thrown out had they fallen into the wrong hands. Only a select few understood the true value of these items.

"Was this from who I think it was from...?!"

Both of them froze in shock and relief, but it was Marin who recovered first. Her eyes were as round as saucers, her brow ever so faintly furrowed. It was rare for her to show her emotions openly regarding something that didn't involve Violette.

"A guy named Chesuit, plus a few others. They asked me to make sure this stuff found its way back to you," Yulan answered offhandedly, enjoying the aroma of his coffee. There was no trace of his icy exterior, either because Violette was present or because he was willing to offer some measure of kindness to people like Marin and Chesuit who treated Violette with care. "If there's anything else you'd like retrieved, I'll pass the message along. They said to tell you the estate is in good hands."

His usual cheery smile wouldn't permit a moment of gloom. He hid it for Violette's sake. She was the type to worry about others first and put her own needs last; whenever someone did something nice for her, her first instinct was to punish herself to make up for it.

She'd had practically no opportunity for self-reflection, and so the line she drew between gratitude and guilt was fuzzy at best. Abuse had taught her to be afraid of any gifts, and because her sense of self-worth was at rock bottom, she reacted not with suspicion but with self-flagellation. Trapped in that house, the innocent little girl had turned herself into an obedient, lifeless puppet in a last-ditch effort to survive.

She wasn't trapped any longer.

"All right, Vio, let's talk."

Let's talk about all the new clothes we'll buy—chosen by you and no one else. Don't worry; you'll look great no matter what you wear.

We won't have our own house for a while, so first let's discuss your room—a place where you can relax in peace and comfort. For you, size probably doesn't matter as much as the amount of sunlight and the view from the window. What kinds of furniture would you like? I thought I already knew all your favorite things, but I never thought to ask you that.

Let's frame an album of pictures so you can reflect on your favorite memories from every angle. Let's build a place together—a life together—and seed it with happiness. Let's talk about our dreams for the future.

I Swear I Won't Bother You AGAIN!

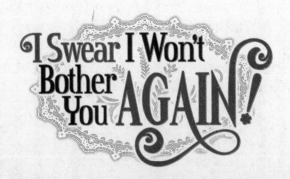

160 | Wrapped around His Finger

"I KNOW YOU were going through a lot last night, but do you remember what I said?"

"Don't worry, I remember."

Tracing her fingertips over her healed cheek brought the memories back clear as day. They stung; she shook her head to chase them away.

Thanks to Marin, the red, cold-chapped skin on her extremities didn't worsen. There were a few small cuts on the soles of her feet, but none of them appeared to be infected. There was no residual mark on her cheek, either; the cut inside her mouth would probably develop into an ulcer, but at least she hadn't lost any teeth.

She was patched up so neatly, none of it hurt anymore. The only thing that pained her now was something she had long considered dead: her heart. The memory held too much emotion for her to compartmentalize it, and until her wounds healed completely, it would only wear her spirit down to try.

"The things you said yesterday...last night...were very sweet and romantic. For me, it was like a dream come true. Truly, it meant so, so much to me...but..."

The events of twelve hours past replayed in her mind unprompted. She was at her lowest point, nearly on death's doorstep, and so clung to the first ray of hope he offered. In her vulnerability, she was completely honest: both that she wanted to be with him *and* that she no longer wanted to live. Marriage could never be entered into as easily as he made it sound, but it was unmistakably something she wanted.

Hailing from a household with no male heirs, Violette was expected to take a husband who would become the next head of the Vahan estate. Granted, Maryjune was more than capable of fulfilling such a task, but it was better entrusted to Violette as the direct descendant of the family line. Not to mention that Auld, as a victim of political marriage gone horribly wrong, would never allow the same to happen to his beloved baby girl.

And then there was Violette's grandfather, the Vahan estate's ultimate authority...a man who prioritized country over family. For the sake of the nation, the duchy could not be permitted to die out. How could she have any say in the matter? A single girl's life was worth less than dirt when compared to the future of the family line.

"I'm grateful that you found me, Yulan. It meant the world to know that you'd look for me. Not to mention everything you said... Really, the sentiment alone is enough."

I'm sorry. I'll be fine. Thank you. She needed to say it with a smile, but her face was too stiff. Not because of her injury but because her hopes had swelled up too large to hide. She wanted to spend the rest of her life with him—she wanted him to make good on the promise from last night, even though she knew full well that they couldn't be together.

"No, Vio. You misunderstand."

He laid a hand over the fists she was clenching in her lap. He was so much bigger now—a man, now. What happened to the boy who couldn't even find his way without her there to lead him? In a blink, those stubby little hands were now large enough to guard and support her. It was so very sweet.

"I meant every word I said to you. I'm going to make all your dreams come true. I'm going to make you happy. Because I *can*."

Only Violette knew of her penitence. Only Yulan knew of his despair. This new future couldn't have existed without the time she spent in jail; he wouldn't have vowed to make it a reality if it wasn't for the hatred that had boiled over at that church. Without the prayers made that day, everything would have been trampled to dust, and that would have been the end of it.

"With you at my side, there's nothing I can't do."

To make Violette happy, Yulan had already overcome time itself.

"In fact, you might even be angry with me for what I've done."

When she fixed him with a puzzled look, he continued.

"You see, er...well, it's a long story, but basically...I kinda arranged some things without your permission...so..."

One minute he was smiling confidently, and the next he was hanging his head like a little boy who knew he'd earned a scolding.

No matter how old he got, this side of him would never change—like the way he peeked up to gauge her reaction, always trying to make eye contact before apologizing, or the way he'd cling to her sleeve until she finally forgave him. Though in this case, he was gripping both of her hands instead.

"Yulan Cugurs, you are completely incorrigible."

As a man, he was her sweetheart; as a boy, he was like a brother. No matter what form he took, he always had her wrapped around his finger...and she suspected he knew.

"Uh...our marriage has already been set in stone, Vio. No one can oppose it—not even you."

"What...?"

"Technically it's a political marriage, I think? I put in a lot of work to convince your grandpa."

"Wh...why would you...?"

Violette wasn't angry—she was, if anything, at a loss for words. She could only imagine how difficult it must have been to persuade a man who dealt strictly in facts, whose loyalty belonged solely to the Kingdom of Duralia, who saw his fellow countrymen as pawns, who felt no sentiment for blood ties. He cared only for the greater good of the nation. Knowing how highly the House of Vahan ranked in the aristocracy, Violette understood what category of pawn she was to him. It would take a tremendous amount of labor and resources to overturn that ruling. So what motive could Yulan have had that would make it worth the trouble?

"Because I want you to take my name."

If it were just about *marriage*, it wouldn't have been nearly as difficult. He could have agreed to take the Vahan name if he wanted an easy way in. Yulan Cugurs had no exceptional status, lineage, or ability, so if all he wanted was to make Violette his wife, then that was all he needed to do. However...

"I'm greedy, and I'm not willing to compromise. I want to marry you, but I refuse to let you stay a Vahan. I wanted it all... and as a result, you got hurt."

She didn't know if he was referring to her cheek or her feet, but neither were his fault—one was her father's violence, and the other, her own impulsiveness. If anything, she was convinced she would have suffered a much worse fate had he not arrived precisely when he did. But of course, whether Yulan would agree was another matter.

In his eyes, he could have done better. He could have resolved it faster, before she ever had the chance to suffer. Instead, he was arrogant and complacent, believing his knowledge of the previous timeline would grant him everything he wanted. It was never going to go perfectly—he was still just a teenager for another year. With most of his life experience centered on pain rather than happiness, he was woefully naive to think he had it all figured out.

"Guess I'm not cut out to be a prince, huh?"

Would the bona fide Prince of Duralia have rescued her more gallantly? Yes, Claudia would have made Violette his princess the *noble* way, with no dark dealings. Sure, he was too drunk on his own sense of justice to see anything beyond what was directly in front of him, but that meant whenever his gaze homed in on someone in need he was inevitably compelled to lend a hand. Yulan could easily picture him rescuing Violette, pardoning the Vahan family, and all of them living happily ever after.

It made him sick.

Yulan could *never* do that. He could take a flamethrower to every one of the people who hurt Violette and it still wouldn't be enough. He wasn't capable of forgiving them—but even if he were, why the hell would he? His seething, murderous hatred would never accept anything less than revenge.

Those people needed to *suffer*—not the swift mercy of death but an accretion of miseries. Something that seemed bearable at first but would eventually make them snap like kindling. That was the misery he wanted to inflict. But if Violette's pain was a direct result of his hunger for revenge...then he should have chosen the harmonious route, even if it cost him his sanity.

"Do you remember that book we read when we were children?" she asked suddenly.

"Huh?"

"We snuck into the library room to read it, remember? The one about the two princes who tried to save the princess?"

"Oh yes, everybody's read it... What was the title again?"

Why did his mouth respond to the change of subject before his brain had the chance to catch up? Did his subconscious mind prioritize talking to Violette over all other functions?

He could remember reading the book with her, but he hadn't cared enough to learn its name. At the time, he'd been distracted by Violette's round cheeks, adorably pink with excitement.

It was a story about Prince Weiss, Prince Schwarz, and Princess Rosa—an ordinary fairy tale of the kind which parents read to their children at bedtime. Neither Yulan nor Violette were lucky enough to have parents like that, and since the book was so popular that everyone else had read it, they were forced to seek it out themselves... The memory felt so distant now. Was that book part of the reason Violette had always dreamed of being a princess?

"I haven't read it since then, but I still remember every word."

After witnessing Princess Rosa's many hardships, the two princes set about trying to help her in their own ways. Prince Weiss chose the power of words. He went around doggedly scolding the people who had hurt her to show them the error of their ways. Prince Schwarz refused to give those people a second chance. Instead, he gave them a taste of their own medicine—including all the passive bystanders and all possible threats to her future happiness.

All these years, Prince Weiss was always the fan favorite. At the end of the story, after he and the Princess were wed, the two of them joined forces to defeat the villainous Prince Schwarz. *He* didn't get to be part of the happily ever after.

"I always wished a man like him would come for me someday... Someone who would burn everything to the ground, just like Prince Schwarz."

She told herself that if she could just endure the pain, some-day her Prince Schwarz would come to rescue her. Everyone would gaze at her with envy as she rode off into the happy ending

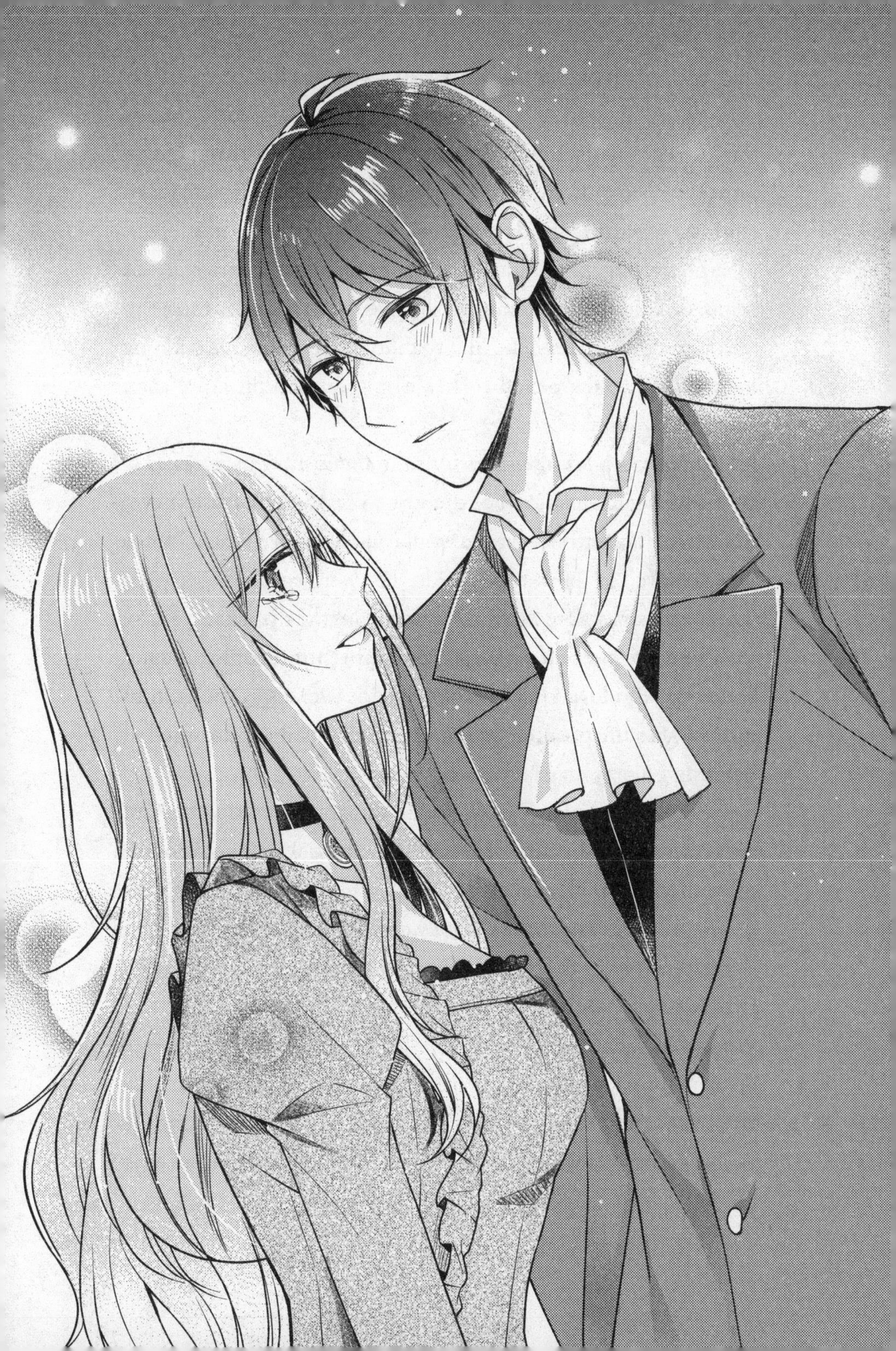

they all dreamed of. She'd wanted Claudia to be that kind of prince, but he only let her down. It felt like a giant flashing sign reminding her that she'd never be a princess.

She gave up. She didn't have the pure, saintly heart of a *real* princess. While she could never forgive her abusers, it took too much energy to hate them. She abandoned that too. It no longer mattered what happened to her. She was nothing more than a puppet, anyway.

It's sad when people hurt you, but that doesn't mean it's okay to get revenge, said the moral of the story. But Violette could never think like that, and so a prince would surely never love her...or so she'd believed.

"I've always wanted to meet a prince just like you."

If not a prince, then a knight in shining armor, or a soulmate. Someone who loved her, who she could love just as much in return. With someone like that by her side, she always dreamed of building a happy marriage—a happy life.

"Thank you, Yulan. Thank you so much... I wouldn't be here today if it wasn't for you. So if you'll be my prince...if you'll make me your princess..."

Then let's get married and live happily ever after, just like in the fairy tale.

162 The Bond of Bloodlust

T HEY WOULD NEVER forget this day for the rest of their lives. There were many more happy days promised to them in a future yet to come, but this was the day it all began—the moment they learned how fulfilling it was to sit, side by side with their hands joined, sharing a smile. It was the first time either of them had ever truly felt thankful to be alive. This day would be engraved in their memories and preserved for all of time. It was the day they agreed to spend their lives together.

⸎

"I anticipate that you'll be staying at this hotel for some time, so I've arranged for you to attend school while living here."

"Thank you... You've gone to such lengths for me..."

"Hardly. I'm just doing what I think is best. I want you to be as comfortable as possible until the house is ready."

Yulan was nothing if not the epitome of thorough. That said, originally, he wasn't going to whisk her away until all the preparations were perfectly in place, so he saw the hotel as little more than a stopgap measure. Violette could only slump her shoulders in grateful shame. As much as it pained her to take advantage of his kindness, now that she hadn't a penny to her name, she had no other choice.

He could tell from her body language that she felt guilty, but he wasn't troubled in the least—if anything, he was delighted to be of service. As much as he would have liked her to rely on him without reservation, he knew it would take time before she was comfortable doing so, and he had no plans to rush her.

"Think you can return to school in time for exam week? If not, I'll let them know."

"Don't worry, I'll be there. I'm in good health now; in fact, I feel lighter than I have in years."

"Glad to hear it. Then let's wait until your injuries have healed. I'll pick you up and escort you there myself."

"Thank you."

In truth, the academy grounds weren't entirely safe. Maryjune would surely try to contact Violette in some fashion, and there was no guarantee Claudia and his associates wouldn't turn on her too. In Yulan's eyes, the only certifiably "safe" person at that school was Gia...and Gia was no ally of his.

"Well, I'd better be going now... Miss Marin, could you join me for a moment?"

"Pardon me?"

The moment he drained his cup, Yulan rose to his feet and set his sights on the maid standing next to her mistress. Caught off guard, she shot him a look of unveiled suspicion while a confused Violette glanced between them. His perfect smile held firm. His voice was flat—not soft or sweet, but emotionless. Rehearsed.

"There are clothes and sundries for you and Vio waiting downstairs. Come and pick out whatever you deem worthy, and I'll have them send it up here."

"Certainly, my lord."

"As for you, Vio, you stay here and rest. Your feet aren't healed yet."

"They're only minor scrapes..."

"Sorry, but when you say something's 'minor,' I'm gonna assume it's a lot worse."

"That would be wise, sir."

"Not you too, Marin!"

Even her most disgruntled pout was adorable to Yulan and Marin. Her feet were indeed injured, and there was no world in which these two worrywarts would overlook it. They would have rather she stayed in bed altogether, but such a constraint would only stress her further. They held their tongues.

More pressingly, each of them wished to speak with the other in private, where Violette couldn't hear, and to exchange information.

"I'll be back again soon, okay?"

"And I shall return shortly, my lady."

Waving goodbye to a smiling Violette, they smiled back with just as much love. Then, without another word, they walked down the hall and stepped into the elevator.

The moment the doors closed, and they felt it begin its descent, the emotion left their eyes in unison. The gold went dull, and the sunset turned to blood, as if the amiable affection of moments prior was merely a trick of the light.

"...So. What is it you actually need from me, sir?"

"Read me like a book, did you?"

"You of all people surely already know Lady Violette's preferences. I can't imagine you have any interest in mine."

"...I'm relieved to know you're precisely the sort of person I estimated you to be."

"Likewise."

They faced forward as they spoke. There was no need to meet each other's gaze for they knew they both wore similar expressions, with similar sentiments, raging at the same mental image. Pleasantries were unnecessary here, and time was short. Between the two of them, they needed only convey the important details accurately and concisely.

"I've told my staff to inform me immediately if someone by the name of Marin calls."

The last time Marin contacted his house, he wasn't there to answer, and it directly led to Violette getting hurt. Truthfully, he had half a mind to fire the servant responsible, but obviously he couldn't do something like that without authorization from his parents. Instead, he decided he'd add it to the list of things to mention along with the engagement.

Furthermore, only he was permitted to contact Violette directly, and all messages for him were to be conveyed at once—not just from Violette but Marin too.

"As I said earlier, I'm going to arrange a few things for Vio going forward. As for you, rather than taking you as part of a dowry, I plan to hire you myself as her personal maid. They could try to use you as a hostage otherwise."

"Right. Shall I submit my resignation a few months prior to the ceremony?"

"I'll leave that to your best judgment. In any case, I'm not sending her back to the Vahan estate, so you could submit it as soon as the new house is ready. I'll only need your signature on the employment contract."

"I see. Either way, it seems I'll need to go back there one last time."

"Let me know in advance and I'll have my staff escort you."

"Understood, my lord."

With most of the preparations already complete, the rest would surely fall into place. Originally, Yulan was going to prepare the house in time for his graduation while Violette stayed in the Vahan family vacation home; her grandfather had granted permission for this along with the engagement. Trust Auld to go and ruin everything. Though it had given Yulan an easy excuse to tear her away from her family posthaste, it wasn't worth the blow to her face. Good thing he'd had the money to pay for a luxury hotel room and a property he could customize.

"You can spread word to other servants if you like, but exercise discretion. I can't have anyone misusing this information to interfere."

"You would be better off asking Chef Chesuit to ensure that instead of me."

Everything in the care package Yulan had brought was picked out by Chesuit and a handful of other staff whose loyalties lay with Violette. Chesuit, then, was in a much better position to foster those connections compared to someone like Marin. She focused her attention solely on her mistress.

But then Yulan lazily lobbed a bombshell into the conversation: "Oh yeah, him? He got fired."

163 Unvarnished Trust

"W HAT...?"

Marin froze. In her shock, she turned to look at Yulan, but his expression was still little more than an emotionless mask. In sharp contrast with her flustered panic, his composure bordered on apathy. Not to suggest she expected him to give a damn about Chesuit's circumstances. As he stood there, leaning against the wall with both hands in the pockets of his slacks, the most he offered in her direction was a glance.

"Surely he didn't *actually* punch that man...?!" It wasn't that his momentary attention had suggested to her that he was waiting for this question—she simply couldn't stop herself from asking.

"What? He announced it to you beforehand? If I'd known, I would have turned up with popcorn," Yulan remarked, his mirthless grin twisted in contempt.

Divorced from context, he looked quite villainous himself. Granted, Marin wasn't about to critique his character, but only because he was an ally to Violette. His sneer would have immediately put her on guard if that were not the case.

"Alas, I'm afraid he didn't punch his master—he threw him."

"He...*threw him*...?"

"I hear the brute was threatening to tear apart Violette's bedroom in a rage. The good chef tried to stop him, but there was a struggle. He threw the man purely on reflex."

Yulan explained it all so casually, Marin nearly found herself shrugging it off right along with him. It couldn't possibly have been as straightforward as he made it sound. In matters of cheer brawn, Chesuit would win by a landslide. Auld was tall and reasonably in shape, yes, but a lean body couldn't compete with one hardened by years of manual labor. Marin had never asked Chesuit if he was trained in any martial arts, but his facial structure and features gave the impression he'd won his share of fights.

That said, when it was employer versus employee, a very different type of power was in play. Under normal circumstances, no one would side with a chef who was violent with his boss, regardless of the reason.

"The incident was swept under the rug, so I'm told there was no formal punishment aside from termination. I don't have the details—it's just something they mentioned when I came to get the care package."

"And...what of the master?"

"...Beats me."

Unlike Marin, whose expression was tense, Yulan showed no sign of remorse. In fact, he looked *relaxed*, like he was in no hurry—like her question didn't even register. This was a lack of regard not for Marin but for the "victim" they spoke of.

"I'm told he hit his head and fell unconscious for a while. He's the one who did the firing, so I guess he must have recovered."

Hard to say whether this came as a relief. While Marin was glad the incident hadn't snowballed into something more dire for Chesuit, it was decidedly *not* the reaction most people would have had upon hearing this news. Blunt force trauma to the head was always concerning at minimum; add in unconsciousness, and some would fear the worst. Not Marin. She was reassured to know Chesuit wasn't punished, but aside from that, it all felt rather anticlimactic.

"If he survived it, then it may as well have never happened in the first place."

"...Right."

There was an element of *disappointment* here. Was it monstrous to feel this way upon hearing of someone's injury? The two of them had so little sympathy for that man—the whole family, really—that his death would never be a tragedy to them. Their bloodlust made them regard him the way exterminators might look at a roach.

"I'm already working on hiring him, so no need to worry about that. Just make sure Vio doesn't hear of it. I'll tell her he resigned in order to work for me instead, same as you."

"I understand."

If Violette learned of Chesuit's termination or her father's injury, she would surely blame herself for it. This was not the mark of a saint but, rather, the trauma of abuse. Every time she was told something was her fault, it taught her to think of herself as the problem. Removing her from her abuser wouldn't change her mindset overnight.

In the past, Violette had fought back hard. The fear of it being her fault made her seek out someone else to pin the blame upon. Unable to endure the self-loathing, she lashed out at others, leading to more loathing and more lashing out—the most vicious of cycles. Yet surely venting her rage was healthier overall than bottling it up inside. Wasn't anger a rational response to being blamed unfairly again and again?

"We are in your hands, my lord."

"I'm honored."

The elevator chimed and came to a stop. Then the floating sensation subsided and the doors slowly opened to reveal the dazzling, spacious hotel lobby. Now that the two of them had exchanged information, there was nothing more to say. No piercing tension—just emptiness, neither comfortable nor unsettling. The perfect silence of unvarnished trust.

"IT SEEMS LORD YULAN really understands your tastes, Lady Violette!" Marin said cheerfully as she returned to the hotel room with several clothing racks in tow, her expression both amused and impressed. Violette frowned in puzzlement as her maid showed her all the finery and accessories, most of them in subdued colors. The dresses lacked volume, but perhaps that was because she was mentally comparing them to the contents of her closet at the Vahan estate.

Everything she'd owned at that house was heavy, constricting, and suffocating—enough to make her gasp for breath while sitting still. The styles emphasized her curves, and yes, she looked very beautiful wearing them. They were designed for the benefit of the *beholder*, not the wearer.

"All of it is well made, tasteful, and the accessories are small and understated."

Marin spread out each one as she organized them for ease of use. Most were dresses with A-line skirts, and none of them had corsets. One set came with a pair of pants, but it looked like loungewear rather than street wear. A few different styles of shoes and bags were provided as well, and the accessories were all hair ornaments—no necklaces or rings.

"He also entrusted me with some funds and asked me to handle purchasing your underthings."

"I'll go with—"

"He said if I tried to leave the hotel, you'd demand to go with me, so he has arranged for a traveling salesperson to stop by later today."

Violette was too stunned to reply.

"It seems he's anticipated your every move, my lady."

As Marin smiled down at her, Violette found her gaze retreating to the floor. Was she embarrassed because of Marin or because Yulan had seen right through her? Surely both. There was something warm and ticklish about it too. For the umpteenth time, she wondered if it was all a dream.

Curiosity was the starting line, knowing was a form of love, and wanting to be known in return was a form of desire. All these conspired to make a crush.

Love inspired people to seek out all sorts of trivia about their beloved—their likes, their dislikes, their skills and struggles, their wishes and ambitions—and to share theirs in return. *I like this but not that; I'm skilled at this but not that; I want to have this, and I want to do that.* In the previous timeline, she flung it all out desperately, wanting to be known, and ultimately, she failed. She never wanted to learn about Claudia because in truth, she didn't love him. Her greed had convinced her that she did, but that was all.

By the time she realized this, there was a new love in the palm of her hand. Something she'd given up hoping to ever receive in return. The days in which she yearned to be with him were so distant that she'd forgotten them. Because she already knew, she didn't realize; because she was already known, she didn't hunger for it.

Oh...I love him...

She always had. Every second of every day, right from the very beginning.

"Would you like to try a few on, my lady?" Marin's voice cut through her thoughts.

"Yes, I think I'd like to see how they fit."

"While we're at it, shall I do a little something with your hair?"

"As you like."

"This is a good opportunity to try something new," Marin offered. "Like pigtails, for instance."

"Oh, Marin, there's no way I'm going to look good in pigtails."

"Of course you will. They're very cute!"

"I'll agree to it only if you put yours in pigtails too."

"I'll hold you to it!"

I Swear I Won't Bother You AGAIN!

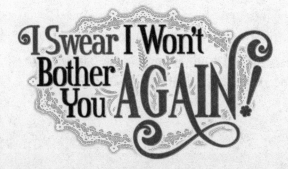

165 | Abscess

IT'S A DREAM COME TRUE. Again and again, the same cliché came to mind. Her happiness was just that magical.

❦

"You're back early, young master."

"Did you tag along purely to poke fun at me?"

"Not at all. I merely thought you'd be gone longer since you were so worried about the little lady."

"And so are you, clearly, since you insisted on driving me here."

As Yulan climbed into the back, Chesuit greeted him from the driver's seat without turning his head. He was a lousy chauffeur—he didn't hop out to open the door for his passenger, and he started the engine right in the middle of their conversation. He was an aggressive driver to boot. Supposedly he'd only ever driven a car to buy groceries for the Vahan estate, so he wasn't trained to ferry passengers. Since it was just for today, Yulan didn't feel like criticizing every little failure.

"Is she doing well?"

"Depends on your idea of 'well.'"

"I don't mean by *my* standards. I mean by yours."

"...Stable, but not in perfect condition. Both of them."

"Can't say I'm surprised."

Chesuit gripped the steering wheel with one hand and rested the other against his chin, his elbow on the window frame. Yulan was, if only technically, a central figure of Duralian society, and yet this man regarded him the same as any other child. He didn't feel the need to walk on eggshells and massage his master's ego with obsequious etiquette. Yulan didn't care one way or the other. He didn't hire Chesuit to be his toady.

"I told Miss Marin what happened to you, by the way."

"Bet she was shocked, eh?"

"She was scared you actually punched him."

"I was joking at the time. Never imagined I'd end up doing something close to it."

"Well, I wish I could have been there to see it."

He would have loved to point and laugh right in the bastard's face. To Chesuit, it was a scandal that cost him his job, but to Yulan it was pure entertainment. Even if it wasn't all that funny, it would have been a great opportunity to scoff at the man's tattered pride.

Indeed, what a shame it was that Yulan wasn't present to witness it. While he was at it, he could have stomped on the bastard's comatose face. Being knocked unconscious was nowhere near significant enough for that man to play the victim card—no, he needed to be ground into paste. Not that it would have sated Yulan's rage to merely beat him.

"So, when do you think I can start my new job?" Chesuit asked.

"Two days from now, if you like. We'll need to start by ordering and arranging the equipment to your specifications."

"Even better. I'm honored you'd ask for my input."

"I'm waiting to see how Vio's condition improves before I bring her in, so that's still undecided as of now. If she doesn't like it, we'll have to start again from scratch."

Yulan's most pressing task was to prepare the house into which Violette would move from the hotel room. If only her pigheaded father hadn't gone on a rampage, Yulan could have taken his time carefully customizing the whole thing exactly to her preferences, but with that off the table, he needed to set up a reasonably comfortable living space as fast as possible. Later, after things had settled, they could brainstorm together to design the perfect castle for a princess.

"It's been so long..."

Yulan's voice was so quiet, it didn't even echo in the confines of the car. With the outcome he'd yearned for right in front of him, he felt no sense of accomplishment. Instead, his voice carried the resignation of one who could see the shadows cast by the light of his granted wish.

He wanted so badly to forget it, but it was always in the corner of his mind, keeping him anxious and on guard. No matter how much time passed, the blade at his throat never lost its edge. Maybe it was merely a hallucination, and the moment it touched him, it would fade into mist—but if it was real, then it was his happiness that would be destroyed instead. And so he was frozen in place.

There was a soft abscess in the depths of his heart oozing blood, so rotten that it would cave at the slightest force. That was where the feeling of loss lingered like a bad infection—something no amount of hard work could heal. It was a trauma he would carry for the rest of his life.

...But I guess I'm fine with that.

As long as he loved Violette, the nightmare of his past would continue to bare its fangs at him. It would target his happiest moments and whisper in his ear to remind him. That was fine—a blessing, even. After all, the terror of losing her was proof of how much he loved her.

166 Our Choice of Weapon

INSIDE THE FORMERLY EMPTY closet now hung a full rack of clothes, all of which were chosen by Yulan expressly for Violette. With the knowledge that he'd thought of her in some way while selecting each of them—the soft texture, perhaps, or the loosely fitted design—getting dressed was no longer a torturous chore but instead something to look forward to. She wanted him to see her wear them. If it wasn't too much to ask, she wanted him to like what he saw. Her heart soared at the thought of him breaking into a smile and telling her she looked stunning. Who knew it could be such fun to dress herself while dreaming of her beloved?

Today was a tiny bit different. Today she would reach for the frock that had previously hung untouched with its garment cover on.

"It feels like an eternity since I last assisted with your morning routine," said Marin.

"Yes, I've been deciding things on my own a lot lately," Violette replied.

As Marin handed her each piece of her uniform, she dutifully put it on, finishing with the ribbon tie. She'd mastered this routine so fully she could do it with her eyes closed and still look flawless. She gave her hair a quick toss and looked in the mirror. Looking back was the same reflection she'd seen every other school day. It felt like ages since she last saw herself in uniform—a lifetime had happened in the time since.

"Now, what shall we do with your hair? With the tools Lord Yulan brought for us, we have quite a few options, my lady."

The past few days had been spent furnishing this hotel room with better trappings than she'd had access to at the Vahan estate. The vanity was covered in beauty products, makeup, and accessories—necklaces to match her clothes, hair clips for lazy weekends, and so on. All of it had met Yulan's high expectations, so it was worthy of Violette by default. Most of all, Marin deeply appreciated having the tools at her disposal to grant any request her mistress might make.

"Hmmm... Let's see, then..."

As she gazed at Marin through the mirror, Violette's expression hardened. It wasn't quite fear—closer to nervousness, but with the steely edge of one who had resolved not to back down, or hold back, or sweep it under the rug.

"Make me pretty."

Violette pursed her lips like she was fighting to keep herself from taking the words back. Next to her reflection, Marin could see her own wide-eyed shock, further highlighting how bizarre the girl's statement had been.

Over the course of Violette's life, everything reflected in the mirror—her eyes, nose, lips, facial structure, skin color, hair texture, and everything else from the neck down—had been praised in some form or another. *Everyone* raved about her good looks. Even Claudia and his posse, who'd despised her in the previous timeline, only ever complained about her personality.

Violette always hated her appearance. Her monstrous mother had only loved her for her face, so she cursed the fact that she was born with it. Nevertheless, she'd lived her life as a beautiful person, and so she knew better than anyone—

"Make me gorgeous."

Beauty was a weapon. The more a girl adorned herself, the more she stood out. In a dog-eat-dog world, that was a formidable tool to have in one's arsenal. In high society, Violette was a born winner, whether she liked it or not.

Had it been that conflict that led to her past missteps? Knowing she was beautiful, understanding the power of a pretty face, her pride had puffed up until it ultimately sank her. Then, in her jail cell, she'd vowed never to bother anyone again. Desperate to be accepted by everyone, she'd sworn to live out her days in quiet modesty. When she discovered the sheer violence of the beauty that plagued her, she'd decided it would only ever be an obstacle to her ultimate goal. Indeed, the Violette from the start of the second timeline would never have asked for *more beauty*.

High society was, in a word, pageantry. Armed with dresses, jewelry, and makeup, women squared their shoulders like soldiers on the front lines, proudly demonstrating their strength to all who would behold it, bravely asserting themselves, standing firm against the weight of their social status. This was not the same Violette who had let her thirst for approval and attention drive her to madness.

Beauty was a weapon of unbelievable power, but most of all, it was armor. She was still so weak—she needed a sword to give her courage and a shield to keep her safe. She needed that strength.

"...Very well." Marin gently parted Violette's bangs, and as her long, slender, faintly calloused fingers rubbed the girl's exposed forehead, she smiled. "I shall draw out every last ounce of your charms until you are truly drop-dead gorgeous."

167 Home Sweet Home

HER SKIN was just bright enough to still look natural—a healthier color than usual. A touch of gloss on the lips, a hint of blush on the cheeks... By sticking to muted colors, her natural beauty was further enhanced, emphasizing only what was already there. Her hair was loosely braided and pinned up with a plain metal clip. It was a simple yet polished look.

The brand-new tools were still foreign to Marin, but she was confident in her skilled hands and discerning eye. None knew Violette's strongest assets better than she did.

"Good morning, Vio. How are you feeling?"

"Very well, as a matter of fact."

"Glad to hear it. Feels like forever since you last wore that uniform, huh?"

"Indeed. You'd think I'd be used to it after all these years... Strange, isn't it?"

"Well, don't worry. You look wonderful."

Slowly, to avoid startling her, Yulan reached out and touched her hair. It was naturally soft, but with extra conditioning and

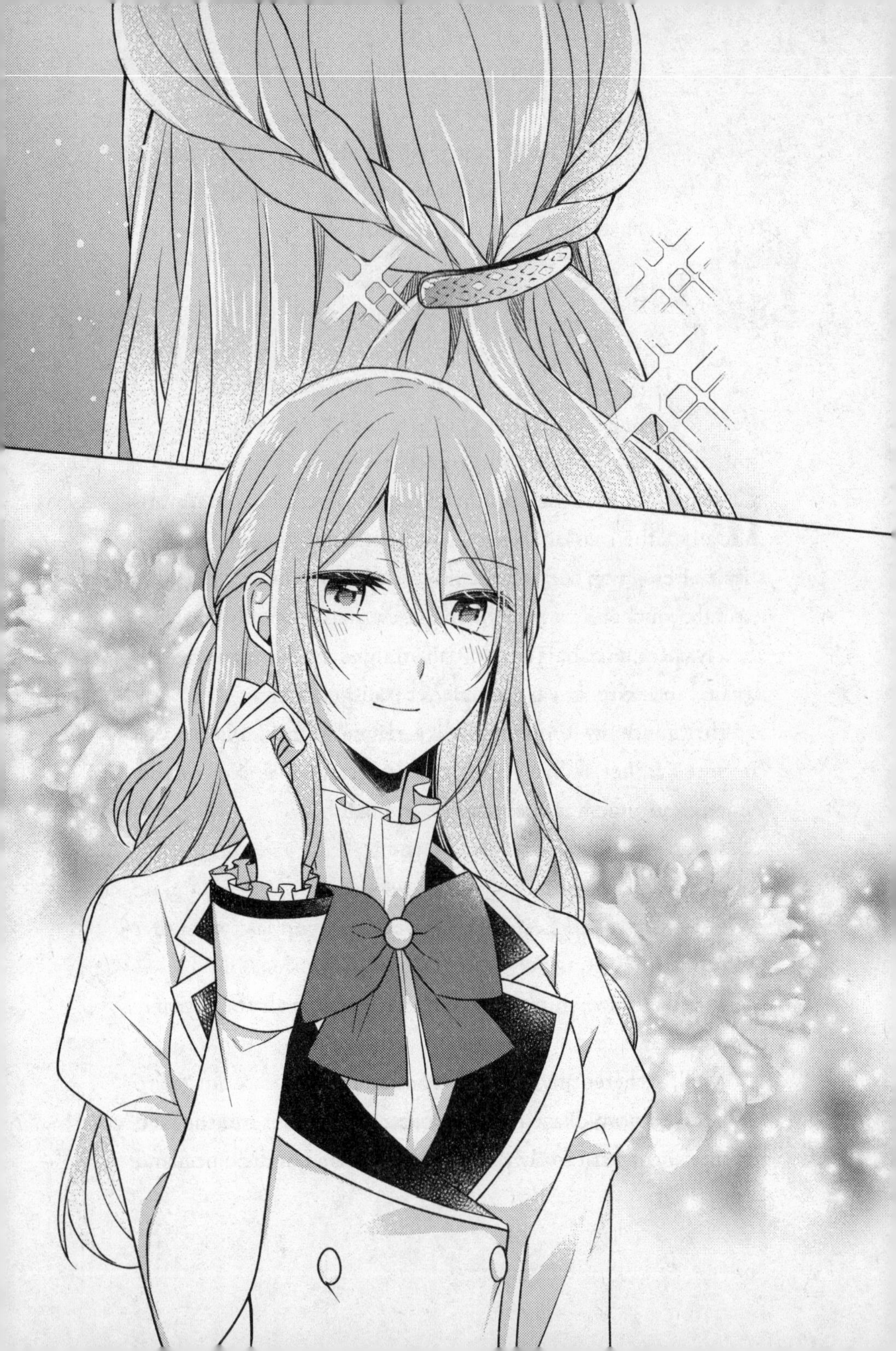

careful styling, it had turned to silk. A golden barrette glittered at the back of her head, at the dividing line of the half updo. He smiled as the pale gray strands slipped between his lithe fingers.

"Beautiful."

His smile was as sweet as cotton candy drizzled with honey. They were locked in their own little world. Marin suspected he'd forgotten that she was standing there...or, more accurately, he didn't care. In his eyes, there were three categories of people: himself, Violette, and everyone else. No matter who Marin was, she would only ever be a footnote. Violette's outlook was hardly different, albeit less extreme, so who was she to complain? All that mattered was the bashful glee on Violette's face.

"Oh...th-thank you. I owe it all to Marin."

Yulan didn't care. To him, Violette was *always* beautiful. He noticed whenever she changed her makeup or hairstyle, yes, but it didn't affect his opinion. She could switch things up or keep them the same—whatever made her happy. His love for her was unconditional.

"I didn't get to give my input on the makeup selection. Is there anything you're missing? I looked it all over, of course, but I'm no expert, so..."

"I wouldn't consider myself an expert, either, but I'd say there was more than enough—even some in colors I've never tried before."

"Well, if there's anything you're curious about or want me to buy, let me know, okay? I'm not gonna notice if it's missing, and I'm sure you'll want to have it on hand for whenever you need it."

"Right... If I think of something, I'll be sure to tell you."

"Good. I'm gonna hold you to that."

One day in the not-so-distant future, Violette would make her official debut into high society. No marriage, even to Yulan, would negate that responsibility as a member of nobility. Once that happened, her mistakes would not be overlooked due to a lack of equipment, colors, or skill.

Her status as a student protected her to a degree, but once graduation day rolled around, that shield would vanish. Violette, and by extension Marin, needed to use this time to hone their craft and judgment lest a single blunder make her a laughingstock in the future. Not only did her garments, accessories, and makeup all need to match, but she was expected to study the ever-changing trends. In that respect, she was already well behind. For now, her natural beauty forgave much, but the clock was ticking.

"Why don't we go browse a little after school today? I'd like to take the opportunity to broaden my horizons."

"Yes, I really ought to study up myself instead of relying on Marin."

"Then it's a date! Wait for me at your desk and I'll swing by to pick you up."

"I look forward to it."

Given that exams were approaching and Violette had missed several weeks of school, one would think this time was better applied elsewhere. If she didn't take steps to rectify her grades, it was obvious what would happen. Then her father would explode with rage—

Just then, her train of thought stopped short. Why dwell on something so grim? For years she'd numbed herself to his abuse, but now she was free from it. It wasn't that she was stupid; it was that his expectations were unreasonable. Besides, after all that studying with Rosette, she could probably get passing marks without much of a struggle.

"All right, Marin, I'm headed to class now. I'll be home by sunset."

"I'll be right there with her, so don't worry."

"Understood. Take care and safe travels, you two."

As Violette gently waved goodbye, and Yulan regarded her with a glance, Marin remained frozen in a deep bow. For the first time, her mistress had said the word "home" with a smile. Marin felt tears well up in her eyes.

———

I Swear I Won't Bother You AGAIN!

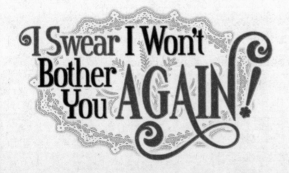

168 Oil and Water

"*GOOD MORNING!!!*"

The moment Rosette laid eyes on Violette, she rushed up, skirts swishing, until she was so close that their noses were practically touching. Her pale eyes sparkled like the jewels that adorned her hair. Violette couldn't help but admire the beauty of Rosette's bittersweet smile, even if now was hardly the proper time.

"Good morning, Rosette. Have you been well?"

"Oh...yes, I...quite..."

Rosette trailed off, nodding over and over, on the verge of crying. Her voice caught in her throat. The few words she managed to choke out couldn't convey her meaning.

Violette didn't know what reason had been given for her absence, but it certainly wouldn't have been the plain truth. On the contrary, he was likely to leave the other students in the dark. This would have been fine if she were only gone a few days, but after several weeks, it was bound to have caused concern.

"I've been doing well myself, actually...so..."

She started to say, *Don't worry, I'm fine,* but thought better of it. It was too late now to pretend things were "fine," and furthermore, it was a disrespectful way to treat a dear friend who had so clearly been worried about her.

"Vio."

After watching the exchange from a distance, Yulan walked up and placed a hand at her back. Before her gaze could drift to the floor, she found herself glancing up at him. His smile was the opposite of the anxiety she felt. Like magic, it melted all her tension away.

"We don't have much time. Why not have a nice chat at lunch?"

"Oh...I see. Would that be all right with you, Rosette?"

"Of course! I'm happy to catch up anytime."

At first Rosette was stunned by Yulan's interruption, but her beautiful smile was quick to recover. This was hardly surprising to Violette. She suspected all that experience being swarmed by the masses had taught the Princess of Lithos how to avoid making a fool of herself.

"Oh, and I'll be joining you, by the way," Yulan added.

"...Certainly. I don't mind."

"Great."

Both of their smiles were a little forced—was Violette imagining things, or was the air heavy between them? Had the two of them even met before? Given that they went to the same school, it was possible they had encountered one another at some point unbeknownst to her. (Indeed they had; Violette hadn't the faintest inkling of just how dramatic that encounter had been.)

"Do the two of you already know each other?" she asked.

"I wouldn't go that far. We had a brief conversation once. Before that, I only ever knew her by reputation," said Yulan.

"Likewise, I knew his name and face, but we hadn't associated with one other," said Rosette.

"Oh, I see... Should I do a round of introductions anyway, just in case?"

"Well, I *am* curious to hear how you'd describe us, Vio..."

Yulan's expression and tone was nothing like the version of him Rosette had met previously. Evidently, he could alter his persona drastically. She could almost believe he was a completely different person. As for which was the real him—neither, without a doubt.

"I'll come get you at lunchtime, so just wait for me at your desk," said Yulan.

"I'll reserve a room for us. Why don't we meet up in the entrance hall?" Rosette suggested.

"...Thank you so much, both of you."

Violette felt guilty that they were going to such lengths...but more than that, she was grateful. Truthfully, she was afraid to be alone. School used to be her safe space away from home, but now she knew what a *real* safe space felt like. Even with all the other people in the building, she couldn't shake the fear in her heart that one specific student provoked in her.

As time passed and she regained a bit of composure, she'd attempted to reflect on that fateful day. She remembered the pretty girl with the tear-streaked face, clinging to her, desperately calling her "sister." Now that Violette was stable, she felt no pity. No affection, no forgiveness, no compassion. As ever, all she felt was a strong sense of disinterest on a foundation of disgust.

169 Trust and Friendship

THANKFULLY, VIOLETTE wasn't as far behind as she'd feared. Her first class in weeks was a simple review of the upcoming test material.

Her classmates snuck curious glances at her, but no one dared to ask her about her long absence directly. She didn't know what they were envisioning, but if they were imagining the usual Vahan family dirty laundry, it would be all too easy for most to fill in the blanks. Bellerose, at the very least, never cared about propriety— otherwise she wouldn't have made her daughter into a son. She never considered how a society that demanded femininity of girls would judge one in boy's clothes and a bowl cut.

"Hey, Vio, I'm here to pick you up."

"Yulan!"

Like the spring breeze tickling her cheek, the mere sound of his voice was enough to lift her spirits. Her thudding heartbeat began to ease. With her beloved right in front of her, she didn't want to waste a moment thinking of anything else.

Just like that, her vision narrowed to just him. It probably wasn't healthy, but it was more freeing than anything she'd felt in a long, long time. She wished she could hide herself away in a tiny little box in that corner of the universe forever.

❧

Once they met up in the entrance hall, the three of them headed to the private room Rosette had reserved at the edge of campus. The room was a corner unit with only one window. While the light fixtures kept the room from being too dark, the man-made light was harsh and unsettling.

It wasn't Rosette's intention to go somewhere gloomy. It was simply the best place for a discreet conversation.

"Why don't we eat first? It'd be a dreadful shame to let the food go cold."

"Good idea... What did you order, Rosette?"

"The avocado feta salad. I tried it for the first time the other day and I've been *obsessed* ever since."

"Oooh, that does sound delicious. I should try it myself sometime."

"It's heaven! Would you like a bite of mine?"

"No, no, I couldn't possibly steal your lunch..."

"I said *a bite*, Lady Vio, not the whole thing!"

"...Well, all right. I graciously accept."

Violette slipped into a familiar rapport with Rosette, as if they'd never been apart. Neither of them were forcing a light conversation. The way she accepted everything with a sweet smile, Rosette was truly the ideal princess. She was also Violette's one and only friend from the outside world.

Where to begin explaining? Even if she left the previous timeline out of it, there wasn't much of her life worth recounting to someone else. What little she had was shot through with triggering memories. She wasn't confident she could skate over them elegantly.

How much does Rosette already know...?

Yulan knew every detail; Claudia, Milania, and anyone else who had known her since childhood could probably guess the generalities. Those from foreign countries, like Gia, would have to rely on what they heard secondhand. In Rosette's case, she'd spent a lot of time networking with other students. If even one of them had let something slip, then she surely envisioned the Vahan estate as the hell it was.

It wasn't just hell, though, was it? For Violette it was, unmistakably so, but for her father and his happy family, it was heaven. That was what made it so difficult for her to speak out. What if Rosette told her she was crazy?

No, she'd never say that...would she?

Perhaps Violette was just desperate for someone to blame. Oh poor Violette, what a victim! Was her "evil" family really at fault? Was she sure she was blameless in all this?

Just because she cared about Rosette didn't automatically mean she trusted her completely. Fear of rejection led to doubt; fear of pain fed distrust. She needed an explanation that would

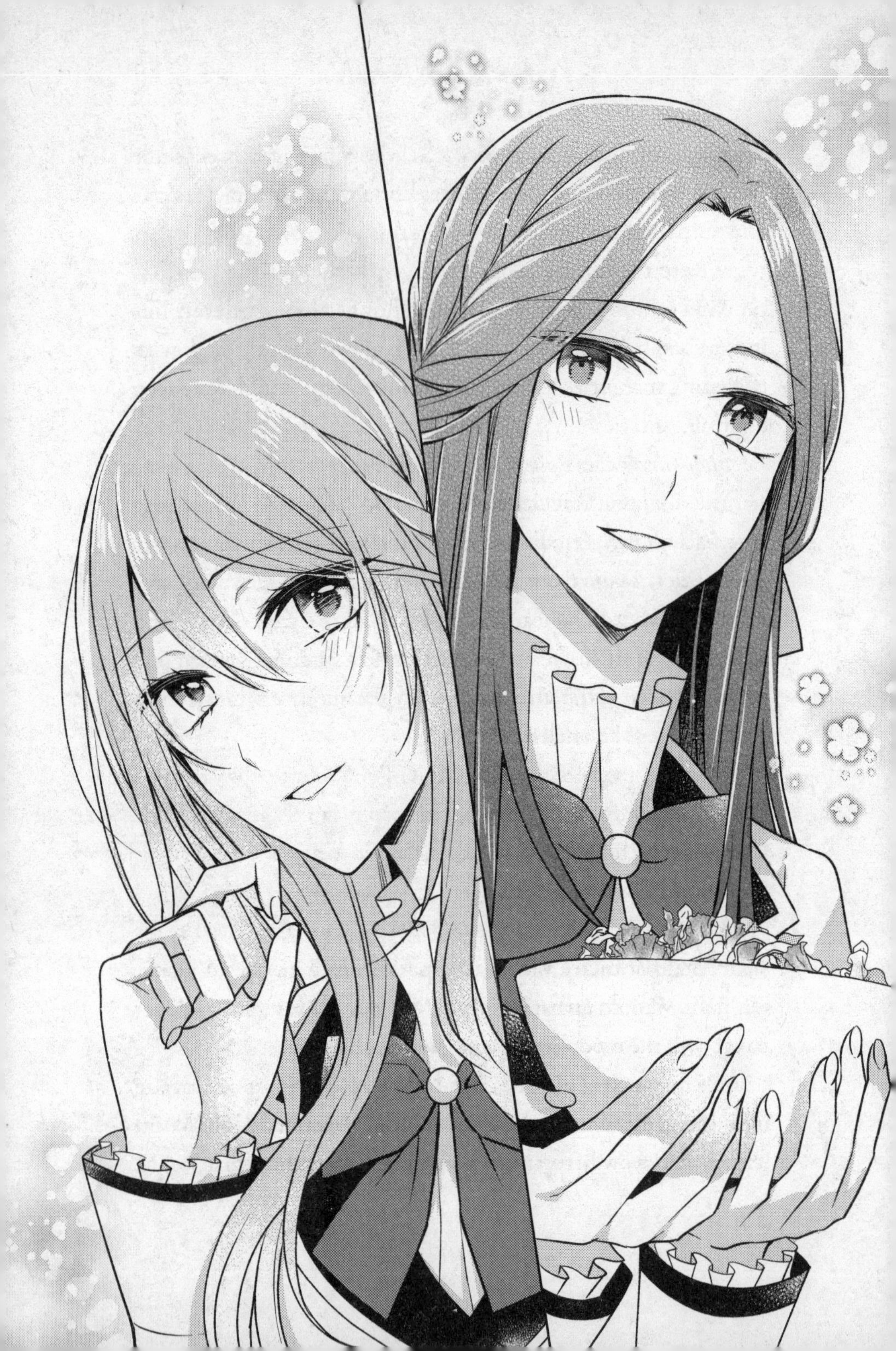

help Rosette agree with her and tell her she wasn't crazy—a turn of phrase to convince Rosette that her suffering was her family's fault and not her own. If she steeped every detail in misery, would it get Rosette to take her side?

When all pretense was peeled away, would Rosette scoff, lose interest, and abandon her?

Her mind was flooded with worst-case scenarios, one after another. She was already imagining the end before it had even begun—not because she was cautious, but because it would spare her the disappointment when those fears came true. If she imagined each betrayal, she could pretend it was her own fault when it actually happened.

Her fork trembled in her hand, making a faint sound as it knocked against her teeth. Rosette merely sat there, smiling, yet Violette was deathly afraid of her. It felt like any moment now, her fears would come to pass.

Her plate was still more than half-full, yet she couldn't eat another bite. She could no longer tell if she was hungry. She couldn't taste her food, and her throat felt strangely dry.

"Lady Vio...?"

Ugh, now Rosette's worried about me. And after she'd made such an effort to keep things from turning awkward... Violette wished she could apologize, but given the subject she was about to broach, the mood in the room was unsalvageable.

As she sat clenching her fists in her lap, a large hand reached over and gently engulfed them. Thus far, Yulan had been a silent witness, but now his warmth revived her frozen fingers. It wasn't a magical panacea for all her anxieties, but it was far more reassuring than trying to have this talk on her own. With him here, she couldn't get cold feet and start lying her way out of it.

Violette didn't need to have this conversation to keep her friendship with Rosette. While telling her the full truth was the best way to repay the worry she'd caused, it wasn't automatically the correct thing to do. In fact, part of her was starting to think perhaps it would be better for both of them if they *didn't* talk about this. But she'd already committed to it, so...

"...Rosette, I need to tell you something."

After this was all over, if it wasn't too much to hope for, she wanted to still meet up and share a laugh in that shadowy gazebo just like always.

170 | No Tears

VIOLETTE TOLD her story. Not all of it. Time was limited, and besides, she couldn't possibly admit to having repeated an entire year. Fortunately, it was easier than she had expected it to be. She could simply list out the sequence of events as if she'd been a dispassionate bystander. Unlike the old her, who could only ever scream about her pain, she now realized that the facts spoke for themselves. If she kept distant from it all, she wouldn't have to relive those feelings all over again.

She spoke about the life she'd lived thus far, about her biological parents, her stepmother, her half sister. About how her hatred for her family eventually wore her down until her heart was numb.

People who'd grown up in a respectable household would never understand. A family was warm and loving—parents were respected, and children were cherished. Everyone parroted such things as though they were universal. While the sentiment was a lovely one, it didn't prevent abuse. The world was full of stories so cruel that they sounded fictional—and not just in society's dark corners. Some of these horrors lived in plain sight, in the beautiful homes of so-called perfect families.

Rosette listened without saying a word. She didn't grimace, but neither did she force a smile. She simply sat there, lending an ear.

When Violette finished telling her story, silence descended over the room until the only sound was their breaths. Rosette's porcelain-white fingers, edged with pink nails, alighted upon the back of Violette's hand.

"Oh, Lady Vio. You've endured so much, haven't you?"

Violette's gaze lifted from Rosette's fingers to her gentle smile—a stark contrast to her own teeth clenched in fear.

"I was always taught that there are two sides to every story. And yes, a mediator's job is to investigate from every angle, not just one."

That was how the scales of justice weighed the good and the bad. To maintain a fair and equal world, it was necessary to grasp the truth. If a third party were biased, the world would tilt to one side, and everything would be chaos. As a member of a royal family, Rosette had a kingdom to protect; thus the king and queen had taught their daughter to view all their subjects through the same lens of impartiality.

"I don't know your family. I've never spoken to them. I'm in no position to decide who deserves the blame."

She couldn't sympathize with the resentment, but...

"But I *am* your friend."

She couldn't step back into the shoes of an unaffiliated third party. Not now.

"I can't turn a gray area into black and white. I can't tell you you're completely right and everyone else is completely wrong. Even so...can you still let me into your heart?"

Regardless of where Violette's feelings took her, Rosette wanted to be right there with her. Rosette couldn't take part in the hatred, but she'd accept whatever Violette chose.

"It must have been so painful, all this time..."

Slowly, Rosette put her arms around Violette. She was afraid the girl might push her away, but she only flinched slightly with no other protest. After a moment of hesitation, Violette lightly grasped at Rosette's arms. It became apparent at once that no one had ever taught her how to hug properly.

"...Thank...you..."

Her voice shook like she was about to cry, but no tears fell. She would only shed those tears for someone who knew the same pain and felt the same hatred—someone who could support her day and night, like the boy beside her. The most Rosette could offer her was her presence.

"Actually...there's something I must tell you as well, Lady Vio."

Violette looked up in confusion. Her eyes were wet, but no tears adorned her cheeks.

There was no deep significance behind the choice to tell her now. Rosette had always been meaning to say it, and this was simply a good opportunity to do so. Now she was confident that it wasn't going to hurt Violette as much as it once would have.

"As of a few days ago, my betrothal has been set in stone...to Prince Claudia."

I Swear I Won't Bother You AGAIN!

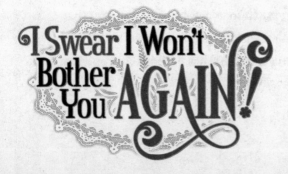

171 Lit Fuse

"**W**HAT...?"

Rosette's tone suggested this was nothing special, but for Violette, it was a dropped bombshell. Not because it marked the end of her notorious, hopelessly one-sided crush. The two of them had privately agreed to bury the hatchet not too long ago, so emotionally, she was fine. But it was, for lack of a better explanation, a jarring conflict with her memories. She struggled to reconcile them.

Claudia was supposed to end up with Maryjune. Violette had been convinced that this was one fact that could never change. With her out of the picture, she was sure this bond would be forged even stronger.

They were supposed to be destined for each other. They were the heroes, and she was the villain—she was punished instead of being chosen. The witch who had tried to break them apart was burned at the stake, and the two of them had lived happily ever after. She'd believed without question that the villainess Violette of the first timeline was destined to meet that end.

"He was one of several candidates—the *prime* candidate, if the rumors are to be believed—so it's hardly sudden, but...the formal announcement will happen any day now."

"I...see..."

She felt a prick of pain, as though someone had stabbed the newly softened flesh of her heart with a needle. Now blood was dribbling out one drop at a time, spreading the stain bit by bit... and the next thing she knew, she was nearly falling apart.

There was a gloom in her chest, a heavy weight on her shoulders, a feeling of discomfort that plagued her. It was not quite nausea, but whatever it was, she wanted to disgorge it. The feeling swelled so rapidly, she would soon risk losing control of it altogether.

It wasn't jealousy. She knew what it felt like to want something so badly she could taste it, and while this was the same degree of intensity, the desire was completely different. She didn't want it for herself. She just couldn't allow someone else to throw it away. This wasn't directed at Rosette, or Claudia, or even herself. She was endlessly, inexplicably frustrated at no one in particular.

You're telling me everything I've done...everything I've felt...

The love that had sentenced Violette to prison...wasn't fate?

She'd prayed so desperately to be loved. When she realized it would never happen, she gave up and learned to embrace the pain. Only then did love finally find her. There were so many things she never would have gained, and discoveries she never would have made, had she not taken this path. So in that sense, arguably, her second chance at life had been worth every minute.

But her scars—her bitter memories of rock bottom, with only misery for company—refused to accept these platitudes.

She'd endured and held back so much, all so she could avoid being a hindrance to the *star-crossed lovers*. How could it end like this? If they weren't going to be together, then what was the point of all the time and energy and pain she'd invested? When she was sent back in time, was their destiny undone along with everything else? If no one could remember the deep cuts from the first timeline, then who was to blame?

"Lady Vio?"

"...Forgive me, I'm just...surprised!"

The pain in her jaw made her realize she was clenching her teeth again. She hastily donned a smile, though it wasn't clear whether Rosette bought it. Frankly, it didn't matter if she thought the smile was genuine or not, as long as she didn't ask what was wrong. Sure enough, while Her Highness *did* look mildly concerned, she didn't dig further.

"Anyway...it seems we're nearly out of time," Violette continued.

"Oh, you're right... It's gotten late, hasn't it?"

"Strange how time flies whenever I chat with you."

"Likewise!"

In the distance, the five-minute bell was ringing, warning them to hurry back to class. Since this room was in a distant corner of the campus, they would need to leave now if they wanted to make it back on time.

At the stairs, the girls parted ways with Yulan; next, in the hall, Violette said goodbye to Rosette and her pregnant silence.

Then, once she was finally, mercifully alone, the smile vanished from her face.

Thank goodness the bell had rung precisely when it had. A moment more and she might have started taking out her messy emotions on her two dear friends who had done nothing wrong. She'd felt so fulfilled earlier. Now everything she saw grated on her nerves—even the feel of the air against her ears as she walked. Her stomach was full of hot lead, and it was slowly welling in her throat.

I feel sick...

What was it that was welling up inside of her? Was this... anger?

172 Howl

VIOLETTE KNEW she was short-tempered. Whenever something didn't go her way, she threw a fit, and she'd resorted to underhanded tactics many times before. Her fuse was so short, she could be driven to attempt a murder...or so she'd believed.

She struggled to identify the emotion in her chest. It was nothing like the panic she'd always felt whenever she was driven to the edge—it was a gut impulse, screaming for them to suffer ten times the pain she'd felt, gnawing away at her good sense until the boundary line started to blur.

"...o...io..."

Now she understood with visceral clarity why people called anger a negative emotion.

"Vio! Don't you want to go home?"

"...Huh?"

She was wide awake, and yet her mind was as fuzzy as if she'd just woken up. Suddenly, a large hand on her shoulder brought her back to the realm of the living. She turned to find Yulan's smile shining down on her.

"School's over, silly. I'm here to get you," he called out, as if soothing a child.

"What?"

At this, she looked around the classroom; sure enough, it was empty save for them. When did that happen? On her desk was the textbook from her first afternoon class, but it wasn't even open. She must have spaced out for more than an hour.

Outside the window, the sky was starting to darken. She typically met up with Yulan at the front entrance, so he must have come looking for her after she didn't show. Fortunately, this had spared her the humiliation of being caught by a campus guard on patrol.

"I'm so sorry, I..."

"Your first day back at school must have worn you out, huh? Maybe you should take a few more days off."

"No, I'm fine. I was just...thinking."

"...Okay."

She averted her gaze while he nodded his assent without prying further, save for a knowing grin. By the time they left the classroom—after he'd helped Violette pack up, of course—he was already back to his usual syrupy smile.

"Oh yeah, I wanted to mention: Gia was worried about you. You should say hi to him next time you see him."

"He was? Not to be rude, but...that's very surprising."

"Yeah, he doesn't especially care about other people. He just noticed that you were absent, that's all."

"Now *that* sounds more like Gia."

While she was a little disappointed that Yulan didn't pry, she was also intensely relieved. The flames of rage were still smoldering in her belly, so hot that it throbbed like a burn. She wasn't sure what sort of spark might make it flare up again.

"He infuriates me," Yulan continued. Violette wondered if he was revisiting that particular memory. His tone was as soft-spoken as ever, but he grimaced as he spoke, like he tasted something unpleasant.

Nevertheless, she could tell that he accepted Gia for who he was. Whenever Yulan talked with Gia, he had a roughness to him unlike what she saw when she was alone with him. Much like how someone could be their true self when indulging in their passions, but also by existing without any facades, Yulan was devoid of pretense around both Violette and Gia but expressed that lack of pretense in starkly different ways.

"Interesting. It's not often I hear you speak about someone like that."

"Oh, uh…sorry, was that harsh?"

"Not at all. If anything, I'm relieved you're willing to open up to me…though I feel bad for Gia."

"Well, you shouldn't," Yulan grumbled, pouting his lips.

Violette giggled. He would surely complain if she told him how cute he looked. Still, it felt like those thorny emotions had been chased out of her stomach. Part of her was relieved just to have put them out of mind.

"Say, would you want to—"

Just then, his words stopped abruptly, replaced by empty silence.

"Oh...? Yulan, what's—"

The moment she followed his gaze, however, her words petered out. A familiar car was parked at the front gates. At a distance it looked like any other, but now that they were close enough to be reflected in its polish, it was clear who it belonged to.

Why would the Vahan family chauffeur be here, if not for Violette? There was only one other.

Without waiting for the chauffeur to walk around, the rear passenger door opened—and at that moment, Yulan stepped in front of Violette, preventing her from seeing who it was. Nevertheless, she knew. She could imagine the petite figure climbing out of the car, like an angel or a fairy, innocent and sweet—a relative who shared a quarter of her blood, who she'd once hated to the point of sororicide, who had worn her heart down to nothing.

"Is that my sister...?"

No matter how harshly she spoke or pushed back, that girl insisted on calling her "sister." Her earnest gaze and pure heart so bravely persisted. And that was all it took to summon back the flames Violette had been desperate to extinguish.

In her gut, a voice howled: *It's all your fault!*

WAS IT ARROGANT to yearn for retribution? An eye for an eye, a tooth for a tooth—a wound for a wound.

"I'm so glad... When I heard you came to school today, I..."

Maryjune's smile was relaxed, as if genuinely relieved. She hadn't the faintest inkling that, with every slow step she took in their direction, Violette was tensing up harder and harder, eyes wide and throat twitching. The sweet angel's voice was poison to her system. She couldn't even be sure if she was breathing.

She felt the same way she had that fateful day.

Before Maryjune could break into a run, a large shadow slid out to conceal Violette. Startled, the younger girl froze and looked up...to find a pair of golden eyes that no longer concealed their disgust with her. Her blood ran cold. The hatred was so palpable, her legs quaked. Her first instinct was to bolt.

Regardless, she stood her ground. "Let me speak to my sister."

"Didn't I tell you? You can't meet with her."

"Please, I just—!"

"Shut your mouth!"

The phrase *shot down* was surely invented for moments like this—an impasse that'd played out, over and over, ever since Violette stopped going back to the Vahan house. Maryjune came to Yulan's classroom every day, asking about her sister and where she was. Each time, he refused to give her a single shred of information. Sometimes she would beg him to the point of tears, only to receive increasingly hostile non-answers.

For the first time in her life, she'd learned just how difficult it was to negotiate with someone who didn't have an ounce of compassion for her. It was frightening and painful. It was *sad*. Maryjune nearly gave in on several occasions, but she couldn't possibly stop; she was afraid that if she did, they would never go back to being a family. Then she would never get to call Violette her sister ever again...

"Sister, I beg of you, please listen to me!"

"............p."

Before she could reach a hand behind Yulan's back, she was interrupted by a whisper. Then, after one or two steps staggered backward, Violette stepped into view. At long last, they were reunited. Violette's expression was concealed beneath her hair, save for one detail: her teeth, clenched so hard they might shatter.

"...ut...up... Just shut up... Shut up, shut up, *shut up already*!"

A murderous glare shot out through her bangs, stabbing Maryjune square in the face. Her brows were contorted so viciously that she looked practically demonic, her beautiful face twisted in unveiled rage.

Maryjune's beloved family had fallen apart, but she thought as long as she kept believing, it would all come back. She thought wrong.

I Swear I Won't Bother You AGAIN!

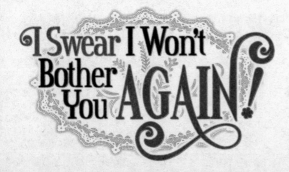

174 Curtain Call

VIOLETTE'S APATHY was maintained by the firm resignation that there was nothing she could do to change anything. After making that fatal mistake in the first timeline, she became convinced that no matter how much she hated this girl, no matter how she interfered, the stupid love story would go on. Now she knew that wasn't true—that in fact, her pain and silent suffering were for nothing. She'd thought that if there was distance between them, she could live with the old scars and fresh wounds...but she'd reached her limit. She couldn't take it anymore.

"You already have everything—a loving mother, a protective father—people who will take your side for no reason—*everything*!"

Her ignited emotions flowed like lava, willing to stop for no one, consuming all in their path until slowing and forming solid rock. Her guilt, her patience, her good sense, her composure, all were burned through—all that was left was boiling fury.

Ah, I see now.

"Would it really kill you not to have *one person*?! What does it matter if I'm gone?! Just leave me alone and stay away from me! Stay out of my *life*!"

Deep down, it was always there, always growing. She told herself she'd locked it up in a drawer, then turned a blind eye to the reason.

"I have no family! *I have no sister!*"

Now she realized she'd been angry the entire time—before she found out the two of them weren't destined lovers, before the day she went back in time, long before she ever committed that crime. If she had to guess, she'd been angry at her entire family from the day Maryjune was born.

While Violette endured her crazed mother's voice day in and day out, *she* was allowed to live happily in peace. While Violette was abandoned by her father, *she* was bundled up cozy in his love, none the wiser. While Violette sat alone in an empty house, unable to cry, *her* tears were fawned over.

"Why me? I…I…!"

What was Violette's crime? Being female? Resembling her father in all but biological sex? Having breasts, bleeding monthly—maturing into a woman? Or was it that she was born of Bellerose and not Elfa, her father's true love? Was it her dull gray eyes and hair instead of sky blue and pearly white? Was it that she was older—that she dared to be the firstborn despite her inferiority? Was it a crime for the eldest daughter of Vahan to be a wicked witch instead of a heavenly angel?

"I…I did *NOTHING WRONG*!"

Was merely being born worthy of such punishment? If she wasn't permitted to ask someone harmful to stay away, if she couldn't ask them not to steal all she had, if she couldn't ask for even the smallest scrap of happiness, if she couldn't ask for love—

"I'm begging you...please, just get out of my life!"

What was the harm, then, in wanting to end it all?

The very sin she thought she'd repented a year prior was now ablaze in irrational anger. She knew she would never be a good person, but this was a level of shamelessness that even she found exasperating. Her crime was not in her motive but in her actions. She knew pointing the finger at Maryjune was only a repeat of the last timeline.

A voice in her ear whispered: *So what?*

Would the punishment for that crime magically erase the motive as well? Did she really think all her homicidal hatred would simply melt away?

Admittedly, she'd hoped for precisely that. Carrying those feelings was painful enough, but once she was labeled a criminal, no one was allowed to sympathize with her. Rather than waiting until it withered and died inside her, she would have preferred that her sentence obliterate it entirely. The unresolved emotional buildup was like a sickness she couldn't purge—it wasn't going to turn into something beautiful.

"I don't need people like you."

For Maryjune, this story wasn't over; the future was littered with chances for things to change for the better. She lived in a world where a bit of effort would lead to a happy ending. For Violette, the door had closed.

Thus the two of them would never see eye to eye. Regardless of what Maryjune wanted, Violette's idea of "family" was over now. She wasn't cutting ties—she'd never had them, so she was choosing to let them go. That was the extent of their connection. Whatever family Maryjune thought she had, it had never existed in the first place.

175 Thief

VIOLETTE HAD LASHED OUT with unmistakable malice, intending to hurt Maryjune. Now that she'd spat out all the bile in her system, intense guilt bloomed in her empty heart.

Maryjune stood there in the aftermath of her sister's remarks, white as a sheet and tragically beautiful with tears flowing down her face. For Violette, the sight of it only magnified her negative emotions. She could feel a stabbing pain in her softened heart, but at the same time, it made her want to scream at Maryjune. She didn't *deserve* to cry. The conflicting emotions made her sick to her stomach.

God, I wish I was dead.

"Breathe, Vio."

"Ah...!"

"It's okay, take your time. There you go. Good job."

She felt a rhythmic *pat, pat* on her back, as if she was a colicky baby. Gradually, her flickering vision began to stabilize once more. Directly in front of her was a button-down shirt, blocking her view of Maryjune's tears. Then her gaze traveled upward, and she found Yulan smiling down at her. One hand remained at her back as the other grasped hers. That was all it took to deepen her shallow breaths.

"You must be tired. Let's go straight home today and get some rest."

It was as if he'd completely disregarded the conflict. If he were truly a *good* person, he would have worried for Maryjune, who looked to be on the verge of collapse. That was the sort of kindness most people were raised with. Since he was different, then he had to be a *bad* person. Why else would he choose the rageful witch over the feeble, crying angel?

It made her happy he was like her. Violette was surely every bit as twisted as he was.

"I bet Miss Marin's got all your favorite treats waiting for you when you get there. And some warm tea too. I sent all kinds of tea leaves, but if you ask me, it's all down to preparation."

His voice was so gentle, his gaze directed so unwaveringly at her, she could almost hallucinate that Maryjune wasn't there. Slowly, he pushed her along, guiding her one step at a time. With his support, her stiff body began to cooperate. She relied on him to avoid obstacles so she wouldn't need to face forward. Her focus was entirely on him—his smile, his voice.

Without missing a beat, he opened the rear passenger door for her. The chauffeur's job, but Yulan was faster. Once she was inside, he put a hand against the door and leaned in through the window. They were supposed to be heading home, but...

"Sorry, Vio, could you wait here for a sec?"

"Huh...?"

"...I need to have a word with her real quick. Can't risk her telling the family about you."

"Oh..."

It had happened only moments prior, and yet somehow, she'd already forgotten the girl's tear-streaked face. Her heart grew heavy as she cursed herself for being so callous; searing pain throbbed somewhere deep in the recesses of her soul. She didn't want him to go. It was her business to take care of. But if she had to see that face right now, she knew she'd start hurling even more insults...and when Maryjune went home with puffy eyes, there was no telling how much mayhem it would cause.

"I don't expect it to take long, but I know you're tired. Wanna go home without me? I can just tell the driver to come back for me."

"No...it's fine, I can wait. I'll wait for you...so we can go home together."

"...Okay. Thanks for understanding."

Violette could hear the amused grin in his voice as she sulkily averted her eyes. She knew she sounded like a bratty child clinging to her mother's leg—as if there was something she just couldn't accept. As he walked away, that childish feeling was the furthest thing from her mind.

Hurry! Please! Please hurry back here, away from her!

This wasn't the restlessness of distrust or anxiety, nor something as cute as jealousy or possessiveness. It was the fear of a serial thief, ingrained in her since the moment of Maryjune's birth.

I Swear I Won't Bother You AGAIN!

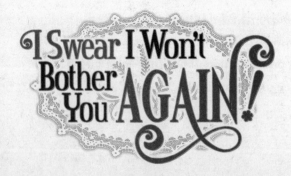

176 | Those Not Chosen

THE SIGHT OF MARYJUNE hunched over filled Yulan not with pity but with irritation. This idiot couldn't mind her own business, could she? Her level of stubbornness was far worse than he'd anticipated. Had she thought he was bluffing all those times he'd warned her? If only she could have recognized it as a kind gesture and exercised some restraint, this never would have happened.

"A textbook example of *reaping what you sow*, wouldn't you say?"

She gasped, flinching almost melodramatically, then froze without turning to look at him. She was afraid of him, sure, but he would argue that if she didn't have the courage to face him, then she should have stuck to being a meek, sheltered little flower. Too bad Daddy Dearest taught her to see herself as special. Clapping sardonically, he walked around in front of her.

"You know, your stupidity is a practiced talent. Congrats! You've got a real knack for trampling all over other people's joy."

She was sitting there white as a sheet, tears streaming from her unblinking eyes. Instead of satisfying him, this only annoyed him further.

She trembled like a prey animal in a predator's clutches, or an angel right before a demon ripped her wings off—unable to run, unable to fly. Granted, this pathetic creature wasn't quite airheaded enough to try to beg for forgiveness. Had she but a touch more self-awareness, she could have saved herself from getting torn to shreds.

"Did you think someone would come to the rescue if you wished hard enough? That all your dreams would come true if you *believed*? Did you foresee an ending with your sister back home and your perfect family back to normal?"

Perhaps it was fitting for a purehearted girl to want to "fix" her shattered family. Yulan had no intention of taking that from her or telling her she was wrong. After all, if she'd been trying to change the Vahan family, he wouldn't have been *nearly* this angry. He might have tried to hinder her efforts out of spite, but overall he wouldn't have had a single scintilla of interest in her. No, Maryjune's mistake was wanting Violette to restore the status quo.

"It must be so much fun to throw stones from your ivory tower. What delicious *schadenfreude*. Sure, you watched your own sister crumble, but hey, every family needs its punching bag! The show must go on! Right?"

"No...I...!"

"Then what were you thinking?"

After seeing firsthand what that family had done to Violette, why cling to her legs and beg her to come back? Why grieve when

Violette declared that she was done? Why proclaim "I love you," only to turn a deaf ear to the "no thanks" in response? What did this girl *want*?

"Why would anyone trust someone who won't sacrifice for them?"

It was obvious that Maryjune would have to choose either her parents or her sister. She wanted to have both, and so she expected Violette to make the sacrifice. She acted like her greed was virtuous, yet she was waiting for someone else to make it happen—a baby bird with her mouth open wide, chirping with conviction that Mother would come along to fill her beak.

Violette pursued love to fulfill her unmet needs, then abandoned it in order to survive. She wanted to end her suffering so badly, she nearly gave up on life itself. A girl like Maryjune, who had never known sacrifice, was simply never going to be able to reach her.

"I was...I just...I love her, and..."

"And because you love her, she should have to tolerate everything you say and do?"

She talked endlessly about love as though nothing could possibly be toxic about it—even though she, of all people, had seen firsthand how one person's love could be hell for the recipient.

"It's not uncommon for love to beget hate. Your love is toxic to her."

To this day, he couldn't forget how Violette looked that night, with empty eyes and a swollen cheek. He'd probably remember it for the rest of his life. At the time, he'd wanted both to kill himself and to set fire to the house that was responsible.

"New word for your vocabulary: *nuisance*. Everything you've ever done has been that. Unnecessary and unwanted."

He crouched down in front of her and gazed into those bloodshot blue eyes. As he recalled, the pairing of gold and blue eyes was once compared to sun and sky.

"Makes you wonder why you were even born, huh?"

Those twin suns narrowed into fearsome crescent moons.

177 | Love Is Blind

HOW MUCH TIME had passed since Yulan went to go speak to Maryjune? A few minutes, at most. For Violette, the wait felt as excruciating as if it were ten times that long.

"Sorry I took so long!"

At last, Yulan hopped into the rear passenger seat next to Violette. The talk must have gone well because he was in good spirits. When he caught her looking at him, he gave a reassuring smile in response. While she didn't know the details, now that he was back, she felt the gnawing anxiety start to melt away.

"Miss Marin's probably getting worried... What about you, Vio? Feeling okay? Tired at all?"

"I'm all right... I've composed myself now."

She'd been sick with dread the whole time she was waiting, but Yulan's presence was like a calming deep breath. Unfortunately, with composure came self-reflection, and the memory of the things she'd said to Maryjune threatened to steal the breath from her lungs.

"I'm so sorry...I..."

What was she *thinking*? Yes, part of her had always dreamed of exploding in that girl's face and blasting her to pieces. Didn't she know all too well what sort of price she would pay afterward?

She wanted to scoff at Maryjune—to point and laugh at how her perfect life had fallen apart at the slightest nudge, collapsing like a house of cards. She couldn't deny there was some gratification in seeing her cry. On the other side of the coin, there was a voice that asked: *Is it really Maryjune's fault? Did I have the right to say what I said? Could it be that she's the victim and I'm the abuser? Did I go too far? Was it even worth getting angry about? Was it my fault?*

"Poke!"

Yulan prodded her cheek with the playfulness of a child— a gesture so wholesome that it stole the gloom right out of her. Startled, she froze, eyes wide as saucers. He trailed his index finger down her face to her hair and began to twirl it around. Normally, being this close to him would make her self-conscious, but all she felt was relief to have him there by her side.

"No, it's not your fault, and no, you did nothing wrong. I know you can't help but analyze it, but what you're feeling right now isn't guilt. You haven't done anything you should feel guilty about."

"Oh..."

"You're just not used to standing up for yourself, that's all."

The closer he leaned in, the more of her vision he occupied. Up close, his handsome face was all the sweeter. Love had a way of making people more beautiful—both the giver and the recipient.

For Yulan, it was twofold: he was handsome because she loved him, *and* he loved her in return. The sight of him was more captivating than any landscape or sparkling gemstone.

"People who don't stand up for themselves tend to worry about whether they're in the right—whether their anger is justified, or if they're lashing out irrationally. They get scared thinking maybe *they're* the real problem. Then they decide what they're feeling is guilt, which means they must have done something wrong. Really, it's because guilt and fear are hard to tell apart."

Every word was as loving as the smile from which they came. He disinfected and bandaged every wound—the old scars, the scabs, the fresh new cuts—and told her that it was going to be okay, over and over, until she was ready to believe him.

"Getting angry is proof that you value yourself, Vio. It means you're listening to your heart. Absolutely none of this is your fault."

Violette knew he was telling her what she wanted to hear. His sweetness was addictive; if she let him spoil her rotten like this, she'd stop maturing. This wasn't true kindness from a morally good person—it was blind validation. So what? Even if she should become so addicted that she lost motor function, so dependent on him that she could no longer walk on her own two feet, she wouldn't care.

This was the love she'd always craved.

I Swear I Won't Bother You AGAIN!

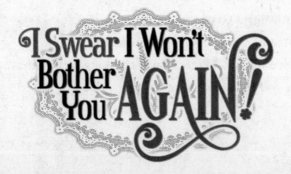

178 | Like Repels Like

To an outside observer it would likely seem grossly overprotective, the way Yulan validated Violette without an ounce of criticism. Praise but no discipline. In fact, a certain princess had once called it a "compulsive need for control." It could be seen as brainwashing—repeating every little thing until Violette believed it without question, acting as necessary to narrow her horizons in the hope that she'd look only at him. The happiness he wanted and offered was wretched.

But with every word, the tension in her body melted away. *Ugh, she's so cute.* The sight of her relaxing filled him with indescribable euphoria.

Violette was a distrustful person—not of others but of herself. That was why she always told Marin she was fine and hesitated to tell Rosette about her situation. Every time she demonstrated that Yulan was the only one she relied on unconditionally, he felt he could die happy. Not that he would abandon her like that.

"Remember that café we went to before? I was thinking we should go again next time you're feeling up for it."

"Oh?"

"I heard they have a new item on the menu. But it's already late, so we can save it for another day."

"What sort of item?"

"I think they said it's a pudding parfait with whipped cream. You used to love caramel drizzled on whipped cream, right?"

"...Yes. I still do."

"Hee hee! Great. We've got a whole week of half days for exams, and after that we'll just coast until the closing ceremony, so we can go whenever you're fully recovered."

"Okay...thank you."

"You're welcome! I look forward to it."

His voice was as overtly sugary as children's cough medicine—addictively sweet but unhealthy beyond small doses. While he would never hurt her, the toxins that built up in her system would inevitably spread to those around her. Like that *worm* of a sister.

From what I saw, she's done for.

At long last, the girl who was born to be loved had discovered the existence of other emotions. She'd learned that, contrary to her delusions, some were born into the world without love or respect or celebration—like her own sister, whose howls of pain appeared to have truly broken her. What would that pompous buffoon think when he saw the state his precious daughter was in? What would she scream about?

If only I could be there to see it. He started to sneer but quickly caught himself before Violette noticed.

Despite what he'd said to the contrary, he didn't mind if Auld found out what happened today. He was even looking forward to how that man might try to fight back. It was easy to picture him rampaging like a bull upon seeing Maryjune's devastation. This time, however, he no longer had a place to vent it.

When he married Bellerose, when Violette was born, when he met Elfa, when he made her his mistress, when Maryjune was born—there were so many opportunities for that bastard to reflect on himself. Each time he chose to dump the responsibility on someone else. Now karma had rolled back around.

Everything Auld wanted, everyone he loved, and everyone he hated—it was his duty to seize his desired outcome with his own two hands. Instead, like a bratty toddler, the idiot blamed it all on Bellerose and Violette, insisting it wasn't his fault...right up until the very moment it all collapsed.

You'd think we were related.

For Yulan, it was like looking at a mirror reflection of himself from the first timeline.

I Swear I Won't Bother You AGAIN!

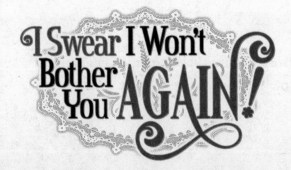

179 Good People

AFTER VIOLETTE had regained her composure and returned to her hotel room safely, Yulan's next destination was decidedly *not* his parents' house.

"Back again, are we, young master?"

"Now that almost everything's been delivered, I wanna finish this project ASAP."

Chesuit spoke as though he was surprised. Considering he'd made enough dinner for two, clearly he wasn't.

This was Yulan's personal residence. It was a beautiful mansion in its own right, and although it was much smaller than the Cugurs estate, it had more than enough space to accommodate a staff of live-in servants. This was where he'd lived as an infant, before his biological mother had passed away. Not that he had any memory of that.

"Well, most of it's ready to go, my lord. All that's really left are the bedrooms."

"Once we put in the bare minimum, I plan to let Vio customize everything to suit her preferences."

Yulan yanked his tie loose with one hand and grabbed his sandwich with the other, devouring it rapidly in large bites. His expression remained unchanged, as if the meal was only a means to replenish his energy.

Over the course of the house project, Chesuit had learned exactly what sort of boy this Yulan Cugurs was. He was never one to be fooled by good looks, but this baby-faced kid had turned out to be more inhuman than he'd ever anticipated. Yulan had no sense of morality. Were it not for the laws against it, he seemed like the type who could kill a man with the ease of saying hello. Chesuit suspected this was because he'd grown up being treated that way himself.

"It's a little late to ask this, but...don't your parents ever ask any questions, sir?"

"This formal language really doesn't suit you. I mean, it's obvious you don't respect me."

"Of course I do. My voice just doesn't carry emotion well."

"It's fine. I don't care how you feel about me if you do your job."

With his sandwich in one hand, Yulan lazily stripped out of his uniform with an arrogance befitting his status. He saw Chesuit not as a fellow human being but an object—a fancy appliance that produced Violette's food. Regardless, Chesuit wasn't going to complain if it made his job easier. And since that was all *he* cared about, perhaps he was just as coldhearted as Yulan in his own way.

"I told them I've promised to take care of her, and I want to keep my word. That was all they needed to hear."

"What?"

"My parents are understanding and open-minded people."

Despite the complimentary adjectives, the boy's expression and tone were muted, like he was reading someone else's opinion from a script. It reinforced the apathy he radiated.

"They did seem like nice folks when I spoke to them."

"Indeed, you'd be right to think that. If you ever need something, say the word and they'll do everything in their power to help you."

Chesuit had only met the couple one time, when Yulan introduced them, and his impression of them was formed largely on their warm voices and genuine smiles. He knew better than to judge a book *entirely* by its cover, hence his choice of words.

"...It's not that I hate them or anything. I *do* think they're good people," Yulan continued after a pause, his voice still devoid of the emotion otherwise implied by his statements. "Morally upstanding citizens, competent at their jobs, loving parents... People of integrity, you might say."

He must have realized that Chesuit could hear the apathy in his voice—and that his word choice wasn't going to convince anyone. His compliments flowed like water, without the slightest hint of negativity, and he truly *did* perceive his parents to be the way he described. So where was the emotion?

"But to *me*..." There, for the first time, Yulan's words took on a heat, though his expression remained eerily blank. "To me...they're the kind of people who never once questioned why I was abandoned."

Yes, the first time this boy ever learned to detach himself was long in the past...

I Swear I Won't Bother You AGAIN!

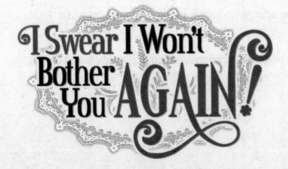

A Shared Sentiment

Y ULAN'S CHILDHOOD MEMORIES were a blur. His first encounter with Violette was clear as day, but the rest of it was shadows in fog. Even the playground bullies had been reduced to silhouettes. Those same boys could be sitting next to him in class, and he wouldn't know it.

Equally as fuzzy was the warmth he felt the first time his adopted parents took him by the hand.

"A competent prime minister is great for his constituents. But for the side that gets thrown to the wolves, he's an enemy. No matter how good his intentions." His competent parents correctly understood that he'd eventually be their problem—hence they adopted the little time bomb themselves and raised him so well. "They're kind people with strong, uncorrupted integrity. They think that by helping someone, it wipes the slate clean."

He remembered the feeling of large, firm, grown-up hands engulfing his tiny little wrists—one soft, one bony—and how they had felt like shackles. Behind their warm smiles, they hadn't the faintest inkling that their new son felt like livestock on the chopping block. They were kind enough to pity his circumstances and competent enough to underwrite his future. They decided to lend a hand. They acted. Even considering their virtues, they were too good-natured to recognize the fragility of the boy warping under their grip.

"Anyone in this country who sees the color of my eyes can instantly imagine where I came from, especially in high society. My parents have only ever insisted that I'm their son...no matter the dissonance created by doing so." If they'd had the good sense to know that Yulan's presence posed a problem for the royal family, then surely they must have known about the scorn and violence that followed him as a young child. "I doubt my life would have been any better if they'd let the son of a prostitute into the royal family, so I won't complain. But I refuse to pretend that no one's at fault."

His parents were always there to soothe him whenever he came home battered. *It's not your fault,* they'd say. *You did nothing wrong.* They didn't realize it was the words they'd left unspoken that gnawed at his little heart.

It's sad, but it's just the way things are. Nothing can be done about it, so no one is to blame. All we can do is try our best to work around it. No one did anything wrong...including you.

"I refuse to let them vindicate the people who victimized me."

They felt that their lazy attempt at consolation sufficed as atonement, so they never bothered to ask Yulan for his thoughts. Not even once. They were kind to him, they cared for him, they helped him—but they never treated the infected wound at the root of it all. That, and only that, was why he had given up on the world.

"Do I sound spoiled?"

Was he a bratty toddler throwing a fit because he'd never asked for the power, wealth, and love given to him? Someone who craved those things would surely resent him for being ungrateful. What else could he say? It was the truth—he never wanted it.

"...Nah. Personally, I'd feel the same way."

"Yeah...I'm sure it'd be too much for you to bear."

Stepping over fences, breaking restraints, following one's heart—as a grown man with unshakable resolve, Chesuit had more freedom than a child. He had the guts to forsake wealth, power, anything that would chain him down. If that weren't the case, then he wouldn't have physically thrown his employer, no matter how much he cared for the daughter of the house.

If only I were more like that, Yulan thought. Maybe then there could have been another way...a way that didn't involve Violette being beaten to a pulp. Then again, if he'd had more backbone, he wouldn't have needed a second timeline.

"That's exactly why I couldn't handle it, sir," Chesuit replied, and when Yulan didn't answer, he continued: "I can offer my support, but I'm not cut out to bear the burden on my own. I can always drop the dead weight, but I can't get rid of *myself*, see? I suspect everyone's like that."

Mere support wasn't enough. This time Yulan had vowed to carry it all on his shoulders. Even if it meant he had to drop everything else. *Everything.*

"The little lady really needs someone like you, young master."

"You think so? Ha ha... I see..."

His voice was feeble, as if on the verge of tears. He laughed with the fragility of a child right before it started wailing like a siren. His cheeks were dry, so one could say he wasn't technically crying. He leaned his head back against the sofa and draped an arm over his eyes, blocking his view of the ceiling.

With his own hands, he'd reshaped his destiny into one where he was good enough. No one would ever know that it was a happy ending to a story that was once a tragedy. He had now tied Violette's future to his own under the pretense of giving her a better life.

There were no tears. He wasn't emotionally moved. But in a split second, that casual, offhand remark had overwhelmed him with such relief that he thought he might cry.

181   Every Pot Has Its Lid

"**T**HIS IS NO PLACE to fall asleep, young master."

As Yulan lay dozing off on the sofa, covered in papers, one would never imagine that his peaceful face was contorted in a grimace mere moments earlier. Most people who knew the boy thought his gentle expression was all there was to him. While he was certainly a master of words and smiles, on the inside, he was a beast.

Organizing the lists again, was he?

Stacks of paper—lists of furniture and daily necessities— covered not only the table and floor but even Yulan's stomach as he lay with his head against the armrest. The house already had nearly everything it would need, and yet the boy still chose to spend his nights sleeping in a room furnished only with cots intended for use by the servants.

Here there was no privacy for Chesuit's meals and breaks. The beds were little more than thin mattresses laid over metal pipe frames, and he couldn't pretend it was comfortable. He'd be lucky if he only had to sleep on it once a week.

As for Yulan's and Violette's rooms, they were furnished with the essentials and nothing more. The master of the house was content with temporary accommodations until the whole place was customized to suit his bride perfectly. The boy was thorough yet sloppy—cautious yet indifferent. It wasn't in his nature to care about worldly possessions...except when it came to Violette.

"Young master, could you at least move the trash to one side, please?"

Chesuit shook Yulan by the shoulder. In response, his brow furrowed. Without opening his eyes, he raised his hand and pointed. Hard to say whether he was awake, but he'd mentioned that he generally didn't sleep well—he struggled both in the morning and at night, and when he *did* sleep, he had nightmares. Chesuit never would have guessed. As far as he'd seen, the boy slept soundly, with no tossing or turning.

He looked in the direction Yulan pointed, where more papers were haphazardly stacked in a much larger pile, almost like the kindling for a fire. This pile hadn't grown for at least two days now, and none of it appeared to have been sorted in any fashion.

"Wouldn't it be more efficient to simply ask the little lady directly?"

"I need to narrow down the options first. If I make her choose at this stage, it'll only stress her out."

Chesuit could picture it all too easily: if someone asked her what she wanted, she wouldn't have a clue, and then she'd feel guilty for not knowing what to ask for. Perhaps the best move was to make it as easy as possible for her to choose.

"...In that case, could you rein it in a little? How can you tell where anything is?"

"Simple. Everything in the trash corner is trash."

"I suppose that does make things easier..."

Yulan had no intention of going back to sleep, because he went back to reading the papers that were on his stomach. At that point it was as though Chesuit had ceased to exist. Rather than risk the hassle of upsetting his new boss, the chef instead set about picking up all the papers that had failed to meet expectations. None of these flyers had personal information printed on them, so he would need to either stuff them in a sack or stack them by size and tie them up. It was easy enough work, assuming he wouldn't have to do it every day.

All the items listed in these catalogs appeared to suit Violette's tastes—as far as he knew, anyway. He suspected his understanding of her was second only to Marin's. To Yulan, however, these things didn't pass muster.

He pays a lot of attention...or maybe he just doesn't spare any for anything else.

The large sofa must have felt cramped and miserable for someone of Yulan's height. The kitchen wasn't yet equipped to make complex dishes, and the plumbing only afforded enough water for a quick dip. While Violette was living like a queen, he'd afforded himself only scraps.

Chesuit glanced at Yulan out of the corner of his eye. Where the boy's expression had been mechanically lifeless during their conversation, it was now animated by a spark of life, suggesting

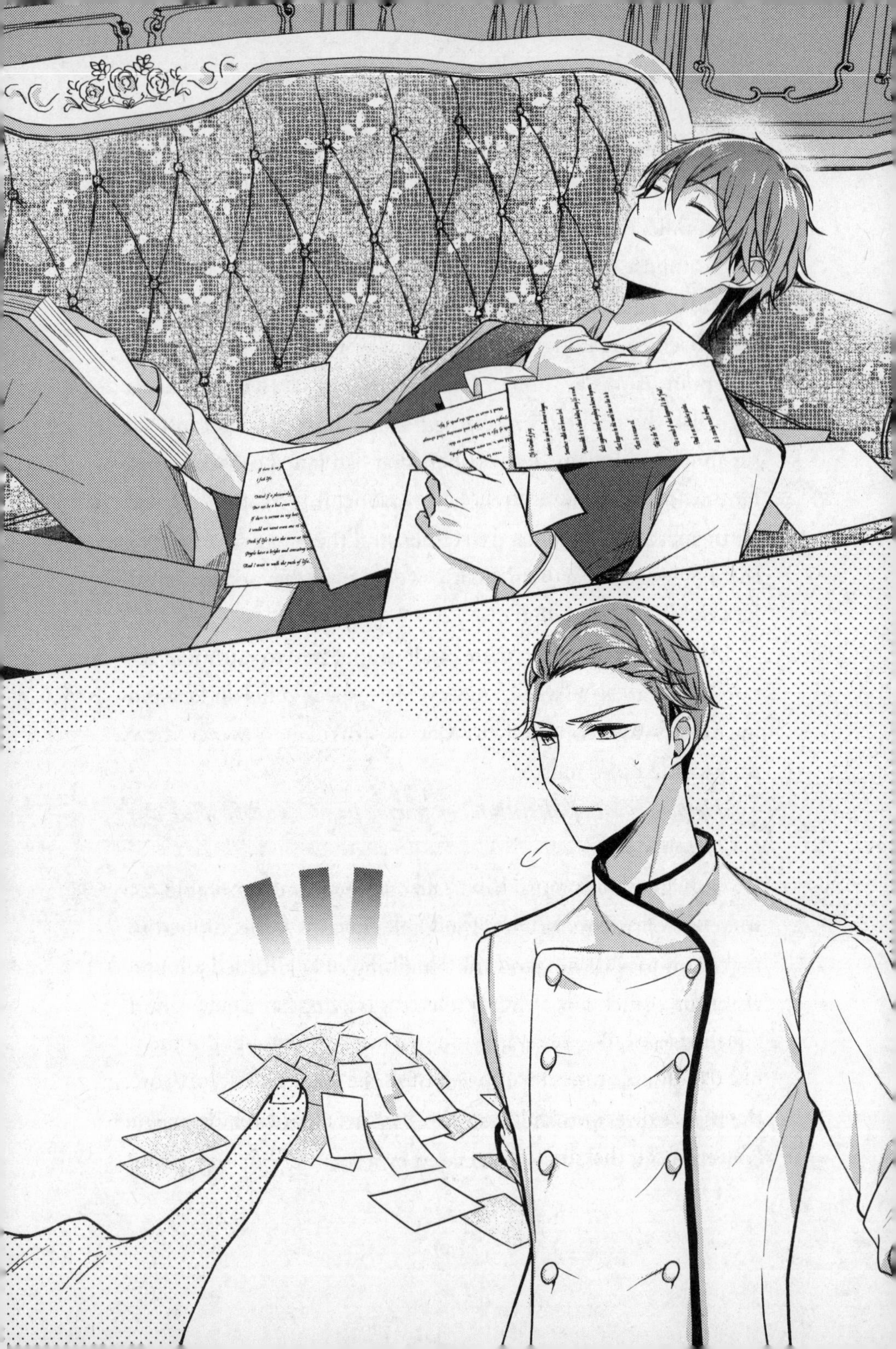
And I want to walk the path of life.

Violette was his sole joy. Their love was twisted on both sides—twisted, broken, and incomplete. But since their devotion was shared, almost as if they shared a single heart, perhaps it could still be called pure.

"Can't say I'm jealous, though..."

"Did you say something?"

"No, sir, nothing."

Yulan was willing to proclaim outright that his life belonged to Violette. While Chesuit could respect that, he wasn't cut out for the sort of relationship that involved being permanently glued at the hip. Most people weren't, if he had to guess.

"Well, I hope you find what you're looking for."

"Oh, I will. Trust me."

"Actually, that reminds me..."

"What is it this time?"

"Congratulations on your engagement."

"...Little late for that, isn't it?"

"I just realized I hadn't said it."

It would have been healthier for both of them if they had never met and developed this sick attachment. At the same time, they surely never would have found happiness without each other. Perhaps it was better to accept their relationship for what it was. Not only did it make Violette happy, it probably made Marin equally happy to witness it—and to a man who thought of them like daughters or much younger sisters, he couldn't ask for more. Besides, Yulan was the type who had no regard for decorum. Chesuit liked that about him.

"Say, if you're awake, could you help me tidy up here?"

"I'd love to, but I'm working."

"You want me to buy that? Try sitting up straight."

182 Burnout

"LADY VIOLETTE, your warm milk is getting cold."

"...Oh, I'm sorry. I was lost in thought." Steam no longer rose from the mug Violette clutched in both hands. Now she could feel the chill of the ceramic stealing the heat from her palms.

"If you're feeling tired, might I suggest you call it a day?"

"No, that's okay. My mind is too awake to sleep right now."

"That's concerning in its own right."

Her blazing fury had been extinguished, leaving behind only emptiness. It felt like a hole in her heart. At the same time, it was because she'd scraped out the last lingering traces of those emotions. Nothing had ended, and yet somehow it felt like everything had.

"Hey," Violette called, "Would you come sit next to me?"

"What...? Er, yes, of course..."

With the flutter of a long skirt, the face that usually hovered above her was now at eye level. Marin sat one seat's width away—close enough to reach out and touch, but a bit too far to feel her warmth.

Back when Bellerose was alive, they would often cuddle up

next to each other in secret, away from the prying eyes of the adults. When was it that they stopped sitting side by side? Violette's life had been so tumultuous, she somehow never noticed.

She scooted one seat over and felt Marin's shoulder stiffen slightly against her own. She knew the woman was simply startled, so she rested her head against that same shoulder.

"Strange, isn't it?" she mused.

"Huh...?"

"With you, I feel at peace."

Violette could feel the warmth of another life beside her. Seeking more reassurance, she pressed her palm against Marin's. This was the hand that made her warm milk, and with every breath, a similar sweet warmth filled her lungs. These were sentiments she would never feel about that house or the people who lived there.

"Try as I might, I can't forgive them...I just *can't*. I don't want to. We don't have that kind of emotional connection."

Maryjune wasn't the only one with delusions of harmony; Violette had dreamed of a family until the day she was forced to give it up. Well, hopefully today would be that day for her sister as well. That was the kindest, most genuine feeling she could offer that girl.

"If I could have said goodbye with a smile, it would have been a beautiful parting gesture. But I couldn't possibly stay calm. I'm too intense for that. It's the one thing I truly have in common with them."

Loath as she was to admit it, she really did take after her parents.

Spoiled, arrogant, self-righteous, always quick to throw a tantrum and take it out on others—like a child in a grown-up's body. Even their actions were identical: resentment had driven Violette to try to kill Maryjune, just as rage had spurred Auld to strike her in the face. Was this something Bellerose had ingrained in her, or was it in her nature from the outset? She no longer knew.

"Perhaps our similarity was the problem. Mother wanted me to be the same as Father, but Father wanted me to be anyone but Mother. I failed on both accounts and ended up somewhere in between. The moment I was born female, neither of them wanted anything to do with me."

If only she were born a boy, she could have been the second Auld her mother had wanted. If only she were born a boy, her father wouldn't have seen Bellerose in her. The instant she was deemed female, she was a failure to both parents—a defective product for disposal. Even if she had been born male, Violette would never have had a happy, healthy life. "He" would have been turned into his mother's plaything or his father's successor and used as a pawn to guard Maryjune's freedoms. No other outcome.

"Frankly, the feeling was mutual. Being their child was an unfortunate mistake. I never needed them in my life."

No matter how the dice fell, she could never be part of that family. They were all fundamentally broken people. No amount of prayer or effort would change that. The only thing resembling a solution would be to cut ties. Leaning against Marin, Violette closed her eyes and let out her emotions in a single tired breath: "I'm exhausted."

I Swear I Won't Bother You AGAIN!

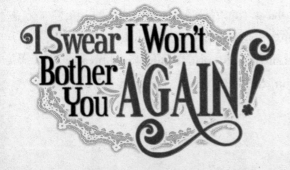

183 Unjust

THE DAYS PASSED without incident. Thankfully, with end-of-year exams to focus on, Violette was free to turn a blind eye to everything else. Each day passed gently: a study session with Rosette, dinner with Yulan, tea with Marin. It was like a pleasant dream—though even in her real dreams, she'd never imagined her life could be this peaceful.

It only lasted until the end of exam week, when Yulan announced that he was going to give his formal announcement to the Vahan family—and Violette wasn't obligated to attend.

"Obviously we can't say flat-out that you're not going. I'll just tell them you came down with something and couldn't make it."

Yulan's frown was rife with guilt, but only for putting her in this position. He didn't care one whit about how rude the Vahans might find it. No surprise there, since he saw no value in going to speak to them in the first place.

Now that he and Violette were betrothed, even *he* couldn't keep ignoring the politics of the situation. He had to consider the optics, particularly from the perspective of the church and the royal family. Flagrant disrespect was too risky. Thus, to ensure his happy marriage, he would wear an unflinching smile for these vermin. He would suppress the urge to stab them in the face. Child's play for one such as him, but he drew the line at subjecting Violette to it.

"You can come see my parents whenever you feel up to it—or if you don't want to, I can explain it to them myself. I doubt our families need to be reintroduced at this stage."

Both families were well known for serving the kingdom of Duralia. Mr. and Mrs. Cugurs were aware of Yulan and Violette's enduring friendship, and in a professional capacity, they had known the Vahan family for years. Because this was a decision Yulan had made of his own accord, he would need to inform both sides.

"I won't be graduating for another two years, so there's no rush."

"Oh, that's right... I forgot you're a year behind me."

"Sure am! But you'll be a third-year soon, so I suppose the timing is right."

Most students of Tanzanite Academy were engaged by the time they graduated, and betrothal announcements happened nearly every day at school. It wasn't unheard of for students to enroll at the Academy with such plans already in place. From Yulan's perspective, it felt like they were running behind.

In terms of timing, it was perfect. Rather than make the announcement at an unusual time and attract unwanted attention, Violette would surely feel more at ease if theirs was lost in a sea of similar proclamations. Likewise, Yulan was content to avoid having to answer a thousand prying questions.

"Even with the two of us sharing a roof, we'll still need permission... Oh, but if you'd rather not, you can keep living here until you graduate."

Auld had yet to say a word about his daughter living in a hotel after running away from home. Either he understood that he was the problem, or he saw it as an opportunity to enjoy life with his precious family. Probably the latter. Yulan strongly doubted Chesuit's throw would have been enough to set him straight, and Maryjune didn't have the spine to stand up to him.

Violette didn't know how different her life would be at Yulan's house versus the hotel, but she could imagine her hypocrite father getting upset that these decisions were being made without his input. This wasn't truly a request for permission so much as a courtesy notice.

"I'm planning to take Miss Marin along, just in case. There's a lot of stuff in your old room, so if there's any furniture or anything else you'd like to retrieve, I'll have it brought to the new house."

The wounds from that fateful day had fully healed, and Violette's face and feet were now just as beautiful as before. Yulan still couldn't shake the image of her shrouded in white bandages. He would never forget who had made her suffer like that.

Speaking of Auld, that idiot likely still hadn't come to terms with their betrothal. How would he react when Yulan turned up on his doorstep? Yulan could envision a few different scenarios, none of which involved a warm welcome. The bastard could spew vitriol for hours at Yulan and he wouldn't bat a lash so long as Violette wasn't there to hear it. Besides, surely she didn't want to have to go back and face the man who beat her.

Violette recognized the generosity in this gesture and appreciated it. Part of her was tempted to agree. But after a pause, a different idea came to mind.

"Thank you, Yulan...but..."

There was still the matter of the scorched wreckage that was her former dreams. Her rage had ignited the kindling, shot those dreams into the air like a firework, and then crashed down. Her dreams lay as ash.

It was hard to put a name to the emotion currently spreading in her chest. After that intense anger, it would be all too easy to overlook something as small as this. More logical. Some might even say to let it slide.

But...

"I'm going with you."

It wasn't hatred or homicidal impulse—nothing so strong as that. Nor was it especially complex. She just felt, plainly and simply, that it wasn't justice.

They don't deserve *a peaceful resolution.*

184 Lull

LOVE, DREAMS, all those beautiful feelings—everything she'd given up on. When she realized they weren't fake, that she could reach out and touch them, that she'd been robbed...the emotion that welled inside her...what was that called?

After the test results were posted, Violette learned that she'd scored lower than ever before. Considering everything else going on in her life, however, it was arguably a victory. If anything, it was much more reasonable than the expectation of perpetually perfect grades.

Her shoulders slumped as she gazed at the pinned paper on the bulletin board. One would think she'd be crushed at her poor performance, but for some reason, it felt as though she could finally breathe.

"Have you checked your results, Lady Vio?" asked Rosette.

"Yes, and it seems I passed. What about you?"

"I did! Shall we go to the dining hall? I hear there's a special entrée today."

"I suspect it's because the closing ceremony is around the corner."

"Ah, yes... It's that time of year already..."

Given that His Highness was graduating this year, the celebration would surely be magnified tenfold. Violette never made it to the closing ceremony in the first timeline, so she could only imagine what it would be like.

"You say that as if you're not personally invested! Isn't your life about to get a lot busier?"

"Considerably, I suppose, but...I mean, it's not like it's *my* graduation."

Following the public announcement of her betrothal to Claudia, Rosette seemed overwhelmed by the level of support she was receiving not just from fellow students but citizens across Duralia. Some had become suspicious of Violette's intentions due to the Claudia connection, but the two girls were both used to the prying stares by now. Violette's own engagement to Yulan would likely be announced sometime later the same year, but it would hopefully go unnoticed in the shadow of the future king and queen.

"I will be taking a long leave of absence to return to my country, during which time I shall take stock of this year's Lithosian jewels, as we discussed," Rosette continued.

"Ahh, thank you. I should seek out a skilled craftsman then, I suppose..."

"The problem is, we still haven't decided what we'll *make* with the jewels."

"True. We only agreed it should be something for everyday use."

"Should we go with hair accessories after all, do you think?"

"We could also make ballpoint pens. With the proper maintenance, they'd last for years."

"Oh, that's an idea. It would make writing letters something to look forward to."

"I would be so pleased to be your pen pal."

So the idle conversation continued. By all expectations, Violette should have felt uneasy. She would soon accompany Yulan to visit her parents. Surprisingly, she'd achieved a level of composure she'd never thought possible. Perhaps the more of a mess one's heart was on the inside, the more it fed a detached, eerie calm.

"When do you expect you'll return?" Violette asked.

"Well...I haven't been home in quite a while, and we'll have to plan the wedding regardless. I intend to take my time."

"I see... Likewise, I suspect I'll have plenty to keep me busy until the start of the new school year. We could arrange an outing after the closing ceremony, maybe?"

"Come to think of it," Rosette mused, "we've never spent time together off campus, have we?"

"With all the exams, I don't think either of us had the bandwidth to think about it. Going forward, we can take our time to brainstorm something as a pair."

"Sounds like a plan!"

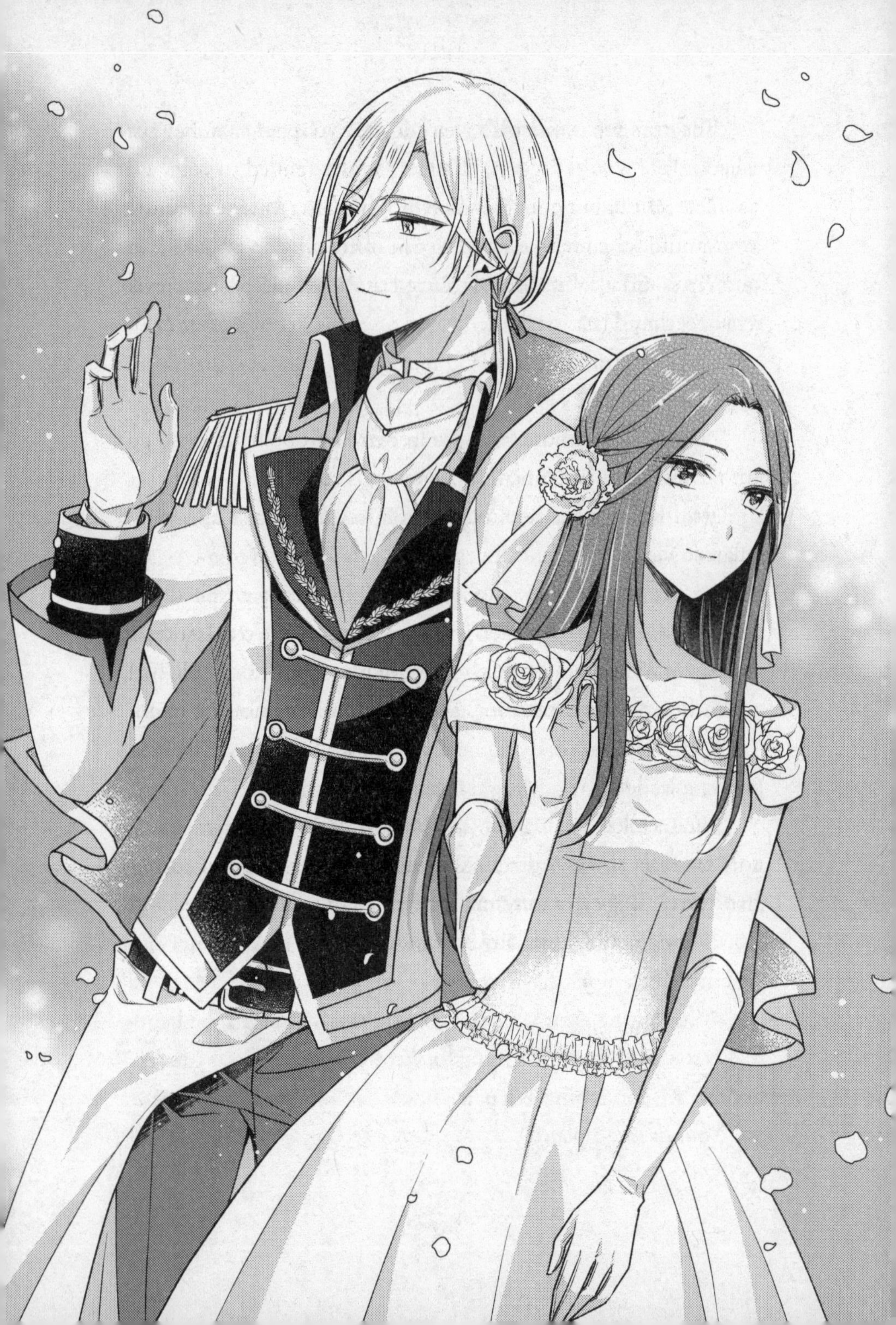

Rosette's soft smile made her look far younger than her polished image would suggest. "Perfect" smiles tended to come off as inauthentic, but this grin only doubled her cuteness. Those who wanted the ideal princess would likely prefer a polished, inauthentic surface, but Violette pitied those people. They'd never get to see Rosette simultaneously master the art of *sophisticated* and *cute* at the same time.

"I look forward to it," Violette replied.

"As do I. To be honest, I've never had an opportunity to go into town the entire time I've been in this country."

"Really? I'm no expert, but I can introduce you to a handful of great shops."

As she chatted with Rosette, Violette dimly recalled the plans she had with Yulan to visit her parents' estate one last time. Because the engagement was her grandfather's decision, Auld had no authority to overturn it. There was no telling how he might lash out. Yulan would be there with her, so she was sure she had nothing to fear.

She recalled the rage on her father's face. His rampage was sort of comical when she looked back. Nothing about it stirred her heart. This was a different kind of apathy from before...and now she vaguely understood why.

I Swear I Won't Bother You AGAIN!

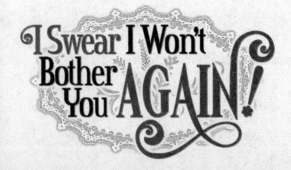

185   Okay

AGAIN AND AGAIN, Yulan asked Violette if she was okay, his expression twisted in concern. When she nodded, he kindly relented, but his brow remained furrowed. Hoping to reassure the worrywart, she looked him in the eyes and smiled. After a long moment, he smiled back.

In the past, the word *okay* was a curse she repeated to herself, but this time she meant it. *She* couldn't explain why she was feeling so calm. The tea he'd prepared for her was strong. By contrast, the memories in the back of her mind were old, faded, and unworthy of comment.

It'd been a long time since she last paid a visit to the Vahan estate, and it was identical to the way she remembered it. A few short months ago she detested the place, but from a distance, she could acknowledge its regal architecture. No surprise there, perhaps, since her mother had dictated every aspect of its construction. Yulan's house was much different, she'd heard, but she'd never even glimpsed it, let alone set foot inside. She wouldn't know.

"As soon as we finish the formalities, we'll go straight to your room to fetch your things. I don't intend to say too much, but just in case, I've sent Miss Marin inside ahead of us to start packing."

"What...? Is that why she wasn't there this morning?"

Marin hadn't shown up the entire time she was getting ready. Violette had assumed her maid was doing some urgent shopping or other work assignment. She never imagined the woman had arrived at the Vahan estate ahead of them. The thought sent a brief chill through her chest. Yulan's next words warmed her back up again.

"Yeah, I sent her with a few of my other staff, so don't worry—she's got plenty of burly men to help her out!"

There was nothing more terrifying to Violette than the concept of Marin entering the lion's den all on her own. Yulan's remark made it sound as though his male servants were there to do the heavy lifting. She could read between the lines enough to guess that they were chosen to serve as bodyguards as well.

"Thank you, Yulan."

"It's fine. I know this morning was probably a bit hectic for you without Miss Marin there... I should have let you know I'd be borrowing her."

"Nothing to be done about it now. No one could have predicted that they'd dictate the date and time without your input."

Yulan had originally planned to turn up to the meet and greet *after* Marin was finished erasing every trace of Violette from that cursed hovel. With Violette herself in attendance, they could cut the visit short with a single sentence: *We're engaged and she's moving out.* That was how Yulan had arranged Marin's schedule—but then that walking personification of arrogance had the nerve to one-sidedly declare a time and date. When Yulan received the letter, he nearly popped a blood vessel. It was only thanks to Chesuit's physical restraint that he didn't show up on the man's doorstep that very night.

"I'm so sorry about him ruining all your plans..."

"You have nothing to apologize for, Vio. If anything, *he* should apologize to *us*!"

It had indeed thrown a wrench into the schedule, but Yulan could look on the bright side: it saved him the hassle of arranging everything else around it. He'd anticipated a stunt like this. Violette had warned him that her father wouldn't take their plans into consideration, and indeed, if the bastard had been capable of it, Yulan wouldn't have needed to take this route in the first place. Expectation was only possible with some level of mutual respect. Given that this imbecile couldn't be bothered to show up on time to the appointment *he'd* insisted on, Yulan added incompetence to the man's long list of sins.

"Remember, you don't have to say a word to them, even if they speak to you. If you start to feel uncomfortable, you can walk out at any time."

"Hee hee! Thank you, but really, I'll be okay."

While Violette felt he was being far too protective, she was grateful that he was willing to compromise enough to let her tag along. Auld was the kind of father who had hit his daughter, driven her out of the house, and hadn't bothered to search for her. She was fine for now. Once he was right in front of her, though…things could change. That was likely what concerned Yulan the most.

Likewise, Violette struggled to explain why she felt so at peace, but she was. Sincerely and utterly okay—even after the man in question walked into the room without so much as a knock.

186 Family

THERE WERE NOW five people in the room, only two of which were smiling. Of the other three, one looked ready to throw a punch while the other two sat with blank, unreadable looks on their faces. Two smiling faces was ordinarily a good sign for occasions such as this one. Under these circumstances, one had to wonder if the smilers were right in the head. There was truly nothing to smile about.

"Thank you for making time to speak with us today."

In contrast with Yulan's sunny smile, Auld was a volcano ready to erupt. He looked ready to grab the boy by his collar. This was confirmation to Yulan that he was right to negotiate directly with the family's oldest patriarch. Though this betrothal was nominally for the sake of political gain, that didn't mean it would lead to an unhappy marriage.

"We've come to announce your daughter's new living arrangement in accordance with our engagement."

But of course, they already knew this.

Yulan's smile was so unwavering, it was like a mask. No warmth or friendliness lay beyond it. It could only be interpreted as condescension. Make no mistake, he *was* condescending to them.

There came the sound of clenching teeth. If looks could kill, Yulan and Violette would both lay dead on the floor. Such was the ferocity with which this so-called "father" glared at his own flesh and blood—his hatred so visibly intense that he looked homicidal. He grew even more enraged when this elicited no reaction whatsoever from her.

It was like looking at herself from the first timeline—the girl who pinned her sister down and raised a knife. His was the same face that was reflected in Maryjune's eyes that night. If only her apple could have fallen farther from this tree.

"Disgustingly poor manners you have, sneaking around behind my back. Clearly, I should have expected it from someone of your background," Auld hissed like a cornered cat.

Only then did Violette's poker face falter. Before she could rise from her seat, Yulan gently placed a hand to stop her, reassuring her with a sugary smile that he was fine. As he turned away from her, that smile twisted into a cold, sadistic sneer.

"I'd watch my words if I were you," he said politely, raising an index finger to his lips as if sharing a secret. This playful gesture was directed at the young girl who looked nearly about to faint. "You'd be surprised to learn how many children are born under similar circumstances."

Like your beloved angel, for instance.

Maryjune lacked the composure to cover her pale face as she teetered on the verge of tears. She didn't seem hurt by her father's statement so much as shocked to be forcibly reminded of her position in society. She believed in her father's love for her without question because she'd grown up with the affirmation of a spoiled, sheltered upbringing. While they may have been a happy family, all that slack had been given to her on a rope tied to a noose.

Even her own father thought of her as a bastard. It was clear immediately that the words Yulan had once flung at her were echoing in her ears all over again, gnawing at her heart. Of all the times for that to pay off! Now *this* was an unexpected perk. Not that Yulan had any interest in the melodrama of Maryjune.

"I admit," Yulan purred, "that my birth could be described as humble. Nonetheless, I'm glad your head of household seems to have taken a liking to me."

It doesn't matter what you think of me, scum. No matter how Auld tried to oppose this arrangement, he could never overturn it. Not just because Yulan had set it up this way, but because Auld himself had thrown away his one means to fight it. This would never have happened if only Auld had worked harder to prove his own worth.

Yulan was little more than the bastard son of a prostitute. Provided nothing tragic happened to his half brother Claudia, his paternal heritage would never be brought to light. He had brought many a tantalizing proposal to win the old man over, but even then, the easiest way to ensure the survival of the Vahan name was for Violette to be used in a political marriage. If Auld

had a more valuable option to offer than Yulan, he could have easily arranged for Violette to be a sacrificial lamb while Maryjune
went on with her perfect life.

Violette's grandfather was cold, calculating, and logical, with
a razor-sharp sense of intuition. But because he was Bellerose's
father, Auld had given him a wide berth. Now he would pay the
price for that miscalculation. In the eyes of a man who was fanati-
cally patriotic, Auld was a mere pawn, keeping the seat warm for
the next generation.

Just then, a set of long, pale fingers rose into the air.

"Pardon me, but...might I say something?"

Beneath this tense air, in a room that might see bloodshed
at any moment, the woman's delicate smile was nothing short of
eerie. This was beyond a failure to read the room—could she not
feel the atmosphere crackling against her skin? Was it a lack of
emotional intelligence? She was unmistakably inhuman.

Maryjune's baby-faced mother turned her elegant smile and,
as if with full confidence that her wishes would be granted, fixed
her unclouded eyes on Yulan—and Violette.

Clearly Auld was a terrible judge of character—and an even
worse student, or so Yulan was told. How could he possibly see
this woman as a beautiful, holy saint?

"Would you not consider taking Maryjune instead?"

187 Love, Love, Love

"WHAT...?!"

The woman didn't even seem to hear the gasps of the two beside her. Her rapturous expression suggested a love even greater than Auld's. Beneath her soft exterior, she was like a snake licking her lips at the sight of her prey. It felt like Violette was coated in slime suddenly, and she reflexively grabbed Yulan's sleeve under the table.

She'd thought she would be okay, and in fact, she hadn't felt a thing—until now. The same resolve that had held firm when faced with her father now wavered as trauma resurfaced. This was something neither Yulan nor Violette could control. This was her animal instincts crying out in warning, haunted by the memory of a wretched mother who had clung to her daughter while calling her husband's name.

"If this is to be a political marriage, then Mary would work just as well, would she not? It strikes me as the more optimal choice, in fact. She's not a Vahan by blood, but she *is* the daughter of the current patriarch." Her smile persisted brightly as she struck every word precisely.

For a political marriage—one where mutual benefit took utmost precedence—Maryjune would indeed be a viable candidate. Since Yulan himself was adopted into the Cugurs family, matters of blood were of no consequence. Thus, if the goal was to marry a daughter of Auld, Maryjune posed no problem. Furthermore, the Vahan family wouldn't have to give up the daughter who carried on the bloodline. Her grandfather would have surely suggested the same himself had Yulan not requested Violette by name.

Indeed, it was the more optimal choice. Logically speaking, it was a win-win for all involved.

"Elfa...what are you *saying*...?"

"You agree with me, don't you, dear?"

Her round blue eyes pierced straight through Auld as he gaped in shock. Whereas before he would have likened them to glittering gemstones, now he couldn't understand how she could smile so widely. This was a man who considered himself a victim of a political marriage gone wrong, as was Elfa in a way. He had been so sure that she, like him, felt nothing but contempt for such strategic unions.

Now, in place of Violette, she wanted to pawn off the sweet daughter they'd so carefully and lovingly raised amidst that very tragedy?

"You must be joking... I'd never offer Mary to this marriage, or this...this *cretin*...!"

He grabbed her by the shoulders as if to shake some sense into her, but her merciful, saintly smile never faltered. Her sweet, soft love had always accepted Auld in his entirety. That was why he'd fallen so hard for her, and why he'd pledged his eternal love for her.

Now a different woman's face floated to the forefront of his mind.

"What other choice do we have, darling?"

As he gripped her shoulders, she laid a hand on his, rubbing it to soothe him. With her dainty lips curled in a frown, she continued, loud enough for the whole room to hear. "I mean...she doesn't even resemble you."

Auld could no longer recall the features of her face—all he remembered was her shrill, unpleasant voice. She vexed him so much, "hate" was an understatement. He'd avoided her at all costs, even when she was on her deathbed.

He had thought Elfa to be the opposite, different from her in every way. When he next looked at her...he only saw Bellerose.

I Swear I Won't Bother You AGAIN!

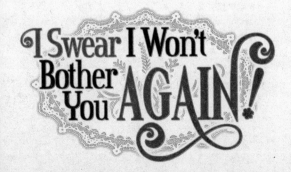

188 Lethal Dose

THE MAN STOOD THERE in wordless shock, staring at his wife and her loving smile—or maybe he simply didn't have the energy to look away. Maryjune gazed wide-eyed at what she thought were her perfect parents, unable to process her mother's words, unable to even blink.

I see what those two were worried about.

Watching this "happy family" self-destruct of its own accord, Yulan couldn't help but be reminded of the two adults who had cautioned him: Marin and Chesuit. The latter had mentioned it before he left the house, and the former had insisted on it very strongly before they parted ways. He had thought his biggest concern would be Auld, or perhaps even Maryjune, but contrary to his expectations, they had warned him of Elfa: the happy wife always smiling in Auld's shadow. Coming from Marin it was one thing, given that she had a strong distrust of the entire Vahan estate. Chesuit's warning was what had raised an eyebrow. It made complete sense in hindsight.

"I see. Are you afraid I'm being cruel to Mary?"

Auld stood there limply, while Elfa grasped his hand and whispered sweet reassurances to chase away all his fears. To Yulan, her voice was so cloying it made him ill, but to Auld it must have sounded like the panacea of angels' song...until a few moments ago, anyway. He'd been given a lethal dose of that sugar. It had started to attack his system.

"Perish the thought! I care for her very, very much. After all, she's your child—your sweet, precious daughter. One who carries your genes, and your blood in her veins."

Her bewitching lips spoke only of love, and every word was the unvarnished truth: she truly loved Maryjune, right from the moment she was pregnant, after her birth, after raising her. Every single second that passed, Elfa had loved her and loved her and loved her and loved her and loved her and loved her and loved her—

"Any child of yours is worthy of my love."

It was an endless torrent that would never run dry, and even then, it still wasn't enough. Elfa loved everything about Auld: his face, his hair, his heart, down to each molecule in his body. She'd cherished his daughter Maryjune from the bottom of her heart. Her suggestion wasn't made with ill intent.

"But certain things must take precedence, and since we have no power to overturn your father-in-law's ruling..."

She smiled sadly, willing him to come to reason. What did she see with those eyes of hers? Whatever it was, it wasn't the blood draining from her husband's face, or the shock written all over her daughter's, or the horror hanging in the air. She was acting so normally, it passed the realm of eerie into terrifying.

This could only mean that Elfa didn't see any reason to be upset. Her idea of family and love...was only ever directed at one person, wasn't it?

"Besides, Miss Violette resembles you ever so strongly. She has your hair, your features—why, she looks just as you did when you were a boy! What a wonderful, sweet, adorable daughter you have. She's everything I ever dreamed of."

Another child with his genes, with his blood in her veins. Unlike Maryjune, this one had his face, and his hair, and...

"Isn't she just *perfect*?"

It was this fantasy of Elfa's, whispered so reverently, that killed her beloved husband's dream with the precision of a blade.

I Swear I Won't Bother You AGAIN!

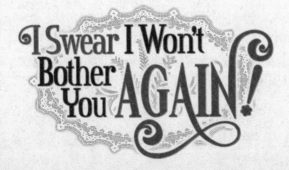

189 The Buck Stops Here

VIOLETTE'S GRIP TIGHTENED on Yulan's sleeve. She was trembling. When he placed a hand on hers, he found her both sweaty and faintly cold. Her lips were pursed tightly, and she was staring at one specific spot in the middle distance, unblinking.

He could only imagine how many long years she'd endured this specific brand of *motherly love*. Her entire life, if he had to guess.

"You don't have to hear it. Or see it. It's okay to close your eyes."

Placing both hands over her ears, he turned her head to face him. As her gaze darted to and fro, he intercepted it with a firm smile. If the traumatic memories were too powerful for her to fight, then he would simply have to pull her out of them himself.

One smile from Yulan and Violette's tense body relaxed. Then she took his suggestion and closed her eyes. Her hands reached up and cupped his, and just like that, she could breathe again. Likewise, Yulan heaved a sigh of relief. With his hands still covering her ears, he shot a sidelong glance at the imploding family.

He had thought of this place as a dollhouse. Instead it was a sandcastle, so easily destroyed with the lightest impact. All trace of it had been washed away; there was no need for him to stomp on it himself. And yet...

There, for the first time since they arrived, his smile became genuine.

"...Well, that's all we have to announce at this time. We shall now take our leave."

Elfa turned to look at him in surprise, her expression so sincere that he nearly burst out laughing. It was as if she was completely unaware that she'd just smashed up her own household. And why would she understand? For her, nothing had changed since the moment she met Auld, years and years ago, long before they were ever married. Only now did the rest of them realize it.

"*She* will be my bride, no exceptions, no substitutions. That was our agreement."

"I see... What a shame."

She slumped her shoulders in disappointment but didn't press the issue further, as if it were no less important than the news that her favorite flavor of ice cream was sold out at the parlor. She would have preferred keeping Violette, the daughter who looked so much like her husband, but she was willing to settle for Maryjune. The one she loved with her heart and soul was Auld—and no one else.

Yulan was tempted to have a good chuckle at her single-minded love crushing the spirit of its intended recipient, but there were more pressing matters at hand. He needed to get Violette out of there posthaste.

"Once we've moved everything out of her old room, we'll see ourselves out. Don't mind us. Continue."

With one arm around her back, he eased Violette up onto her feet. Although she seemed a bit calmer now, her complexion was still ashen, and he felt the chill of her skin through her clothes. He turned his condescending smile on Auld, who looked to be in even worse shape than his daughter.

When he found Elfa, he must have thought he'd escaped from Bellerose. Being with her surely felt like living in paradise. After all, any woman who offered love without strings attached would seem like a saint in comparison to a jealous monster. Everything he'd loved and everything he'd despised—in an instant, it had all imploded into one person.

What was running through that smooth brain of his? If Auld were even halfway intelligent he could extrapolate what the future would look like. He no longer had a scapegoat for his failings. Violette was done being his punching bag. He was finished.

"I'm sure the three of you have *much* to discuss."

God, how I've longed to see that look on your face.

I Swear I Won't Bother You AGAIN!

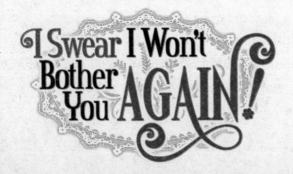

190 Vent

"**H**ow are you feeling? Perhaps bringing you here was a mistake."

"I asked to come with you, remember? Besides...I expected this."

The moment they arrived at her old room, Violette collapsed to her knees. Yulan hastily guided her to the sofa, where he rubbed her back until she stopped shaking. She asked for warm milk, so Marin dashed off to the kitchen. Yulan's servants all remained on standby, waiting for their next orders.

Violette's smile was weak but not as stiff as she'd feared. She hadn't expected to react so strongly to her trauma replaying right before her eyes, but she'd made the decision to come here, fully aware of the possibility.

"I always knew they were similar. That's why Marin's afraid of her. Not to imply that I'm not, but...to Marin, my late mother was the most frightening thing in the world."

A mother who saw her husband in her daughter, and so... loved her like she would a man. It was heart-rending enough to put into words, but to witness it with no means of intervening had been as damaging to Marin as it was to the direct victim, Violette—even more so, perhaps. She knew what life was like on the outside and could compare that to the hell they'd lived in. Long after Bellerose's death, she still haunted them.

"I knew it wasn't a good idea. I knew chances were high something bad would happen. Those people will gut you without a moment's hesitation...and I knew it would hurt. Even then, it wasn't enough to deter me."

When was it that she first started growing her hair out? Or started wearing dresses? Or stopped deepening her voice? She didn't transform completely the very moment her mother cast her aside. Acting like Auld had become a part of her daily life by that point. Hardly surprising, considering it was how she was raised—how she was forced to live. Then she was told it was unacceptable, and now here she was.

Her father had rejected her boyish haircut and clothes and voice. He decided it was inadmissible and corrected it. First Bellerose had deemed her a failure. Then the very man her mother had begged to see again told her to change every aspect of herself. He had determined there was no value in the cross-dressing charade if it wouldn't appease the witch, so he rejected everything about her and told her to be a lady.

So she was. She changed herself *again*. And even then, it wasn't enough.

"I didn't want it to end like that. It's not fair! After all the effort I had to put in to meet their demands...they got to reap

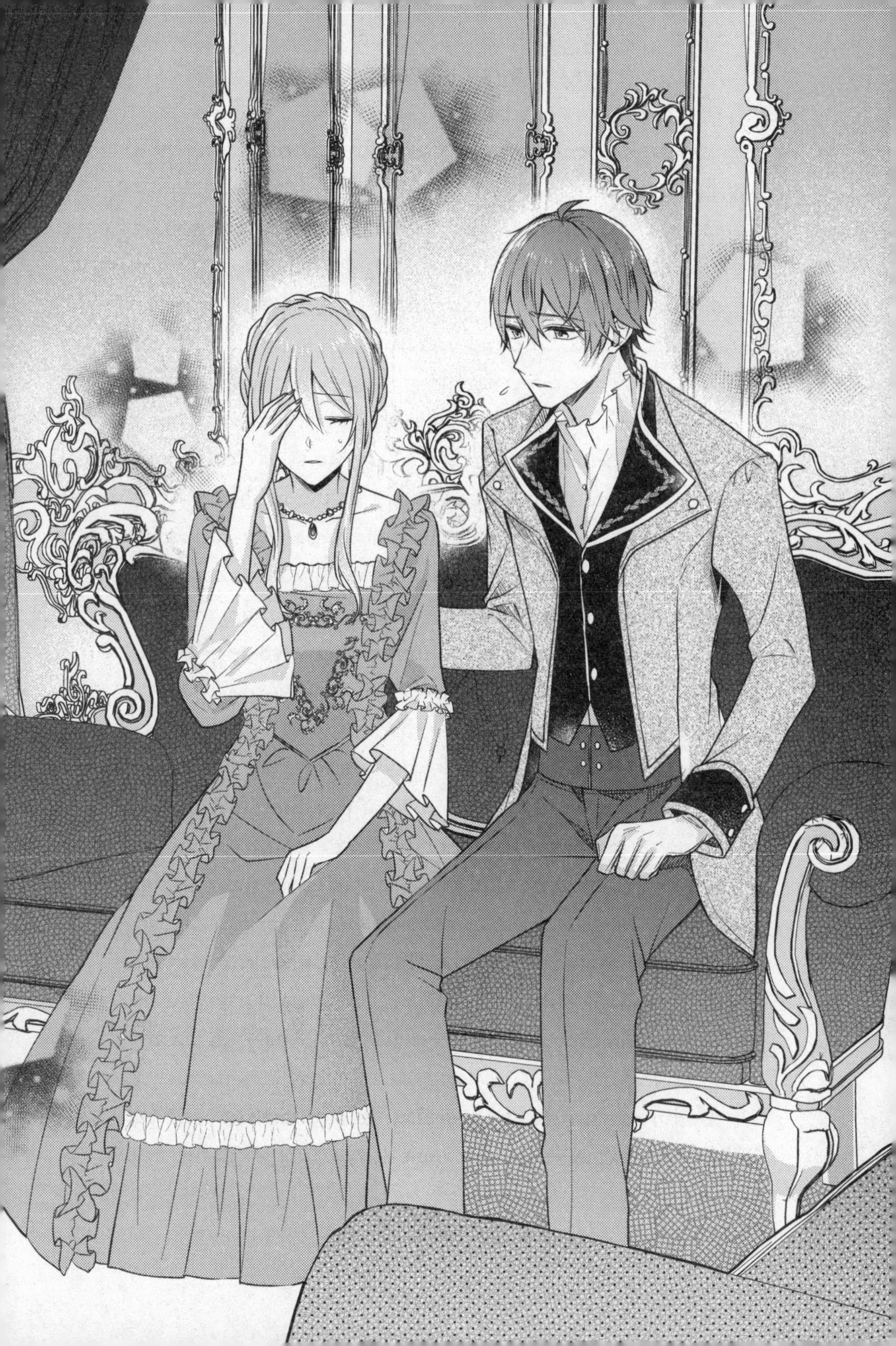

the rewards? I suffered and toiled and *still* never got a damn thing out of it. So I…"

I want it back. Every last thing I ever gave to you people.

"I wanted to see them suffer for a change."

She didn't care if it hurt, if it ripped open her scars and poured salt into her wounds. She wanted a front row seat to the carnage.

Violette directed this monologue at the floor. Her tone and word choice were all over the place, as if wrestling with a flurry of emotions. The damage of reliving her trauma was surely more severe than she realized. Yulan listened to it all without a word. She was free to say whatever she liked, even if it was incoherent. He just wanted her to vent. Bottling it up with a smile had already caused her enough suffering for a lifetime.

"I'm sorry—I didn't mean to worry you. I was so sure I'd smile the whole time. I thought I'd laugh in their faces."

"I'm gonna worry about you either way, Vio. Not because of anything you did, but because that's just the kind of guy I am."

These lunatics were so unreasonable, Yulan didn't feel the need to adhere to any sort of decorum. He and Violette had arrived at the specified time and made the announcement as tradition dictated. For that alone they deserved an award.

"You must be exhausted after all that. Once we're done packing, we can take the rest of the day off! I'll buy your favorite cake on the way home."

He pulled her into a gentle embrace, patting her on the back. He felt her rest her forehead against his shoulder with her full weight, as if she were burying herself into him. With her face concealed, she might have appeared to be crying. He doubted she was now. She had a way of holding her tears through any pain.

"You really tried your best, and I appreciate that. It's okay now. Let's go home."

"Home...yes, home. Thank you."

"Any time."

He scooped up a strand of soft hair and kissed it, and somewhere roughly north of his heart, he felt her smile.

I Swear I Won't Bother You AGAIN!

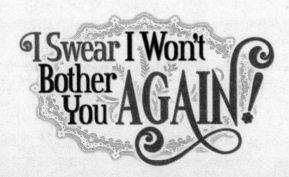

"M MNNH... Oh crap, I overslept again."

Gia had only intended to lay in the shade, but he must have dozed off. Ruffling his hair, he scanned the shadows for signs of life. Nothing had changed while he was out, so the five-minute bell most likely hadn't rung. Class didn't appear to be in session yet. A staff member would have come looking for him if it had, and in a place like this, he would have been discovered in seconds.

"Blegh...I'm thirsty."

He stretched his arms wide, quickly discovering that his back and shoulders ached a little. No amount of freshly landscaped grass would make the ground any more comfortable, he supposed. A bit of light stretching solved the issue, so it wasn't serious.

More pressing was his dry, itchy throat. Come to think of it, he hadn't grabbed a drink with his lunch today. All that food in his belly must have absorbed the water from his body.

"Guess I'll go get something..."

Sluggishly, Gia rose to his feet and retraced his steps back to the dining hall where he'd recently purchased a mountain of food.

"Yo, can I get a drink?"

At the entrance stood a butler, to whom he directed his lazy request. He didn't care what kind of drink it was—tap water would have been fine—but at this school, even the water was served in pointlessly ornate goblets. In the past he used to drink right from the faucet, and only stopped doing so at Yulan's, er... *violent* insistence. This was an improvement. Probably.

A short while later, he received a glass full of sunny liquid. Orange juice, the butler explained. Ignoring the rest of the man's explanation about *organic* this and *100 percent* that, Gia took a sip. Very sweet, but light and crisp. *Yeah, that'll do.* "Thanks, pal."

Glass in hand, he turned away and felt a sharp glare pointed after him. Drinking on the go was considered poor etiquette, so nobody was supposed to do it on campus. Given that students from Sina never got the memo, it was little wonder that they were treated with disdain.

What else was he supposed to do? He needed to get back to class; he didn't have time to stand there and listen to stupid juice trivia. Did *anyone* at this school care to hear it?

He tried to recall what his next class was. If it involved traveling to a different classroom, he was fairly sure Yulan would have mentioned it. Since he hadn't, it probably meant there was another boring lecture in store for them.

I bet it'll happen any day now...

Lately Yulan had seemed sleep-deprived and about 30 percent angrier than usual. Gia was aware he was executing some plot or another. It was all rather amusing. The boy would soon get exactly what he wanted.

"Two more years..."

Gia conceded that he'd enjoyed himself longer than he'd expected to, but the entertainment would only last a fraction of his remaining time here. He had never outright asked Yulan to detail his carefully penned script, but he could tell they were approaching the climax of the story...and once it was over, he would grow bored.

This escapade had afforded him a full year of entertainment thus far, but he was still obligated to attend school in this country for two more years. If he didn't find something else to amuse him, he would rather risk his life jumping the border to get out of here. If he was going to die of something, he'd take a bullet to the back over boredom.

"Gah!"

He was so distracted envisioning this prison break that he missed a stair as he was climbing the staircase. Fortunately, he only staggered forward a bit before his superior athletic reflexes kicked in to restore balance. With a sigh of relief, he looked up to resume climbing—

"Excuse you."

A low, demonic growl came from directly behind Gia, and at precisely the same moment, he realized the thing he was carrying was now conspicuously missing.

"Oops. Nice catch, Yulan."

Liquid dripped from the other boy's hair, soaking his jacket with a citrus fragrance. In one hand Yulan held the now-empty glass, upside down, having taken the full brunt of its contents. His pristine persona destroyed, he glared up at Gia, brimming with bona fide homicidal rage.

"I am gonna kill you."

"Ha ha ha! My bad!"

This glib apology intensified the glare by 50 percent. Gia *was* genuinely sorry for it and *did* feel responsible, but at the same time, a guy like Gia Forte couldn't help but see the humor in it. *You're just too funny, man.*

To someone with no concept of worldly attachment, this walking personification of obsession—the boy who'd kept him amused over the past year—was fascinating. Gia didn't care if the ending to this drama was happy or tragic, but he was dying to know how Yulan's life would play out from here.

Nothing was fun about this country. Too much peace and harmony for his liking. But rather than while away the time lamenting his boredom, Gia had somehow found something here at school worth looking forward to every day. He could only wonder how long it would last.

AFTERWORD

HELLO AGAIN! This is Reina Soratani. Reaching Volume 4 has been a dream come true for me—thank you so, so much!

When I first started drafting this story, I never imagined it would continue for as long as it has. Remember when I thought this was going to be a rom-com? Reading this volume in particular, you'd never guess. It feels more like the big reveal of the final boss.

I developed Elfa's character relatively late into the process. My original plan was that she and Chesuit would rarely ever enter the picture, so all they needed were names. The rest was left completely blank. I only started thinking about Auld and Elfa when I planned out how Yulan and Violette would end up together.

Due to her father's influence, Maryjune is rather shortsighted and oblivious. She never once noticed what was happening to Violette. Since she spent her whole life in that environment, I do feel what she's become isn't her fault. That doesn't mean Violette has to forgive her, even so.

Elfa, however, knowingly slept with a married man, had his child, and became his second wife with no thought for his previous family. No matter what excuse Auld may try to make, he should have felt that something was off. There's no way he didn't notice, right? The moment I realized she could be the villain of my story, I went with it immediately. She's great at provoking Violette's trauma, and she crushed Auld under her heel. I think she's filled her role fantastically. Definitely the scariest person in this series.

As for Auld, I'm sure many people were hoping for him to get his just deserts, but I hadn't planned for that even before Elfa was in the picture. Reconciliation was always off the table, but more than that, I couldn't imagine Auld ever feeling any sort of regret about Violette. I was starting to think she'd never get to taste revenge, the poor thing...but that was when Elfa fell into my lap! What a blessing. Sorry about your trashy taste in women, Auld.

The most fun I had was writing Yulan's dark and twisty side. With Vio he's like cotton candy dipped in honey, but with Maryjune he's an unfeeling demon. It's such a blast! Poor Maryjune's probably traumatized for life now. The princely boy she thought she knew turned out to be a heartless monster—for a sheltered angel, that's a horror story. I felt bad for her as I was writing it, but rather than hold Yulan back, I let him destroy her. Fun!

Considering what a demon he is, it's amazing to see Gia brush off his attacks so easily. I like that their relationship exists in this gray area between friendship and chew toy. That said, while they each have an accurate assessment of the other, they don't truly *understand* each other. Perhaps "friendship" isn't quite apt—more like two people who find themselves stuck together against their will, possibly their whole lives.

I also think Yulan and Chesuit balance each other out nicely. Their rapport is like the one he has with Gia, since Chesuit is a fiercely independent sort of man. He's also one of the few adults Yulan respects. They've only just started getting to know each other, but I think they'll get along. I think Yulan needs someone who can put him in his place every now and then. He's not used to being treated like a child, and regardless of the delicate considerations over status, he might find it refreshing not to be worshipped for a change.

Reflecting on Volume 4, we still have plenty of trials for our cast of villains to overcome. Not just for Violette, obviously, but for Maryjune—rough, painful trials. She was always going to have to learn the truth eventually, and now she's seen her mother's true colors.

As for Elfa, the instant I thought of her "She doesn't even resemble you" line, I knew I had to put it in! I had Maryjune take the blow along with her father. It was gutting for Violette too, in various ways, but she's got Yulan and Marin to support her. I'm not sure how Maryjune and Auld will recover from this, or if they even can. Eventually I'd like to write from all three parents' perspectives, but I suspect nothing good can happen in those chapters.

Anyway: Yulan and Violette are finally affianced! Now that they're entitled to be as lovey-dovey as they like, I can picture

Yulan becoming unstoppable. I'd love for them to go on a double date with Claudia and Rosette, but considering everyone's complicated feelings for each other, I'm not sure it's prudent.

I'd also like the opportunity to give Claudia and Rosette their time in the sun. I do think they have a nice chemistry together; I sense that they'll have a polar opposite kind of romance from Yulan and Violette. We're approaching the final act of this story, but there's still so much I want to write—ah, what bliss! I'd love for you to stick around through it all.

Volume 4 wouldn't have been possible without all the help I received from so many people. Thank you from the bottom of my heart! Like I said in Volume 3, I'm so incredibly delighted and honored to have made it this far. Also, Volume 4 of the manga adaptation is out now. I'd love for you to check it out. As with previous volumes, it includes a bonus short story, so look forward to it!

Reina Soratani
May 2022

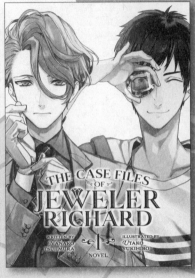